MISTLETOE DREAMS

Mistletoe Meadows
Book 7

JESSIE GUSSMAN

Acknowledgments

Cover art by Covers and Cupcakes
Narration by Jay Dyess
Author Services by CE Author Assistant

Listen to the unabridged audio for FREE performed by Jay Dyess on the Say with Jay channel on YouTube. Get early access to all of Jay's recordings and listen to Jessie's books before they're available to the general public, plus get daily Bible readings by Jay and bonus scenes by becoming a Say with Jay channel member.

Books in the Mistletoe Meadows Sweet Christmas romance series:
1. Sleigh Bell Dreams
2. Icicle Dreams
3. Sugarplum Dreams
4. Christmas Dreams
5. Holly Jolly Dreams
6. Candy Cane Dreams
7. Mistletoe Dreams
8. Silent Night Dreams
9. Candlelight Dreams

Chapter One

"I'm really hoping we can open the clinic on Saturdays now that you're here," Dr. Terry Landis said to Dr. Hannah Reynolds.

Hannah nodded her head. "Although, I understand that you also need to slow down some," she said, eyeing Terry's stomach with a lifted brow.

Terry gave a guilty smile. "I know I need to. My husband, Judd, has been awesome about helping with the children, but this is our third child in three years, and I really don't want to miss these years with them."

"Nor should you have to. That's what I'm here for." Hannah put a hand on Terry's shoulder, and Terry smiled gratefully. There was a tightness around her eyes and dark circles beneath them that bespoke the extra hours and long nights she had pulled trying to keep her clinic solvent and trying to keep her family happy. Also, the pregnancy had taken a toll on her as well.

Hannah was thankful that she had been able to take the job, since Terry seemed like a really sweet person and would be easy and fun to work with.

Unlike her last, exceptionally high-pressure job.

A sour feeling started in her stomach, and she tried to pivot away from going back down memory lane. Although it was not easy. When someone made a monstrous mistake and was threatened with a multimillion-dollar lawsuit, a person had a tendency to not forget.

Not that Hannah wanted to forget necessarily. She did not. A person could always learn from their mistakes.

But those had been some of the darkest days of her life, and not just because of her own problems. She hadn't wanted to make a mistake on anyone's medical care. No matter how honest, sincere, and well-intentioned the mistake was.

"For now though, take the weekend to settle into your new place. I don't think you told me where you were staying." Terry clicked off on the ipad she had been sharing with Hannah and pushed back away from the desk, so that they could make eye contact as the computer powered down.

"Several years ago when my grandmother passed away, I inherited her house." She paused for a moment, thinking about all of the memories that were entangled with the house and her grandmother and Mistletoe Meadows. She'd spent many happy summers here. And in fact, she and Terry had played as children. But that had been a long time ago. "It's in desperate need of some cleaning and some repairs as well. I was here over the summer taking a look at it when I applied for the job. It's livable, but it needs work."

"If you need any help, let me know."

"I will. It's nice to know that I have people in town I can depend on, but I'm probably not going to bother you unless I really need to. You look exhausted."

"I could go for some sleep," Terry admitted. "But I think once you get settled into your new position and the townspeople get used to you, I'll be able to take a bit more time off."

"Hopefully before the baby comes." Hannah lifted a brow but didn't probe further.

"She's due right around Christmas," Terry said, as though she could read Hannah's mind.

Hannah had wondered but didn't want to ask.

"Once we get settled in, we'll have to talk about my maternity leave. I have several thoughts in mind, but I definitely want it to be something that works for you as well."

"Fair enough. I don't think I'll have any trouble getting my bearings. Everything looks fairly straightforward, and you have things very well organized."

"And the people are awesome. Not just with visiting the clinic, but with helping out too. It's not just me that would help you if you needed it unpacking. Most people are excited about the new doctor in town."

"I'm excited to be back in Mistletoe Meadows. I loved spending time here when I was a kid visiting my grandmother. I never dreamed I would actually live here one day."

That was an understatement. She'd always thought she would go to the big city and have a prestigious practice as a doctor in a large, possibly teaching hospital. She hadn't really understood all the ins and outs of the medical education that she would have when she was younger, but she certainly hadn't pictured coming back and working in a small clinic in a tiny town.

Right now, though, that sounded like just what she needed to get her life and career back on track.

"All right. I'll meet you back here Monday morning, and we'll have you shadow me for the first few days to see how things go. Then, when you're feeling pretty confident, we'll discuss scheduling."

"Fair enough," Hannah said, as Terry pushed her bulky body to a standing position and waddled to the door, which she opened for Hannah.

"There are plenty of things to get involved with, if you're interested," she said by way of conversation as they started walking out of the clinic.

"I definitely would like to get involved in the town," Hannah said. But she also knew she had a tendency to bite off more than she could chew at times. Although she really thought the best thing she could do was to stay busy. Was she going to stay here for a long time?

It was a question she didn't have an answer for. But just because she wasn't quite sure how long she'd be in town didn't mean that she wasn't going to help wherever she could.

"There's a town meeting for organizing the Christmas festival. We're actually more on the ball this year, and we're beginning to organize in November rather than waiting until the last minute the way we usually do."

"From what I hear, whether you organize last minute or not, the festival is a hit throughout the state."

"That's part of the reason we're beginning to organize earlier. We're expecting a record turnout this year. We've had some unexpected publicity and a lot of interest, despite the fact the calendar says it's still early."

"Well, good for you then. It's always good to be prepared."

"I agree. Anyway, you're welcome to attend, and if you feel better going with someone, you're welcome to come with me."

"I appreciate that. I might feel a little bit weird walking in by myself, so it'd be nice to walk in with someone who knows what they're doing."

"I wouldn't go that far. It might be more like the blind leading the blind, but it's always nice to have someone beside you when you don't know what you're doing."

"I couldn't agree more."

They talked about the date and the time and made arrangements for Hannah to go to Dr. Terry's house to meet, and then they'd arrive at the meeting together.

Hannah left feeling like not only did she get a good job, but she made a friend. Terry Landis seemed like a very down-to-earth, friendly, and sweet woman. And if the busyness of the clinic was any indication, the townspeople loved her.

Hopefully, Hannah could learn from her and be just as beloved by the town.

Chapter Two

*H*annah walked into her grandmother's house. No, *her* house. It was hard to think of it as anything but her gram's.

She breathed deeply of the air that still seemed to be dusted with cinnamon, although there was definitely a musty smell as well.

She'd just arrived that morning, unloaded a few things from her car, and went straight to the clinic.

Now, looking around, it was obvious she had a lot of work to do.

The U-Haul with most of her things would be arriving the next day, although she had no furniture. The antiques her grandmother had used were still scattered around the house and had conveyed when she had inherited the structure.

She smiled at the worn, old-fashioned couch where her grandmother had sat with books on her lap, a cup of tea steaming on the coffee table, while they spent Saturday afternoons reading together.

Although the kitchen was where most of her memories had been made. The Formica countertops, the old-fashioned linoleum floor, and the cupboards that looked like they had been made out of plywood during the Second World War were gently worn and serviceable, but would never win any fashion awards.

It could definitely use a remodel, but Hannah wasn't sure if she was interested in that. After all, the things as they were held a lot of memories and made her happy. What did she care whether it looked modern or not, as long as it was functional?

A little scratching sound alerted her to the fact that she might not be living in the house by herself. Her skin crawled a bit as she thought about what a person needed to do in order to get rid of a rodent population.

Suddenly, the idea of sleeping upstairs held less appeal.

She pushed her shoulders back. Most likely those were descendants of the same mice that lived there when her grandmother was alive. Not that she held any fondness for the family line. Still, it reminded her she needed to finish doing the laundry so she had clean sheets to sleep in.

After she switched the laundry, throwing her sheets in the dryer, her stomach growled, and she realized that she hadn't done any grocery shopping at all.

She had been in such a big rush to get to the clinic to... revive her career? She wasn't sure exactly what she would say, because that wasn't the reason. There was no reviving the career trajectory that she had been on in this small town. That had hit a sudden and very harsh dead end.

Grabbing her keys from where she'd left them, she focused her thoughts on the here and now. Get enough food to survive the weekend and fuel her body while she unpacked and settled into her new home so that she would be ready on Monday morning to tackle this next challenge in her life. She was no stranger to doing hard things, having survived medical school and residency and landed a job at a prestigious hospital in the city, and she supposed this was no different.

Still, she hadn't anticipated what had happened and figured that there was probably no way that anyone could.

She turned her car onto the main street of Mistletoe Meadows and drove down the familiar, nostalgic road, passing the park where she and her grandma had played when she was younger and then entered the downtown area with streets lined with small shops, including Henderson's candy store, as well as the candle shop which had always smelled so good, and the other cute stores.

As she headed toward the new grocery store on the other side of town, she noted a policeman standing along the road, talking to two rather scruffy-looking teens.

The policeman looked stern but kind. And there was something familiar about him. Or at least there seemed to be. Hannah had known a good number of kids from town, although she'd never gone to school with them because her parents had lived just outside of Charlottesville, and she'd only visited her gram in the summer, over school holidays, and the occasional long weekend.

She would've moved in with her if she could have, but... maybe her life would've taken a different turn. She really didn't know, and speculation along those lines was a waste of time.

The warm glow from Henderson's candy shop made her smile, and her heart warmed as she watched a lady wearing a hairnet seem to teach a young girl how to pull candy as they smiled and laughed together. A man, handsome and wearing an apron, lifted a brow at their antics, watching as he dumped something into a mixer, and the whole family just seemed so cozy and happy and represented everything that was missing in Hannah's life.

Deliberately. She'd made deliberate choices, knowing that she was going to miss out on some things because she wanted other things. Unfortunately, those other things had been yanked away from her, and she was left with nothing.

Should she have made different decisions?

She drove by the church, noting the well-used parking lot and a couple of teenagers shooting hoops in the deepening twilight.

Eventually, she made it to the grocery store and pulled into the parking lot, which was almost deserted. She had forgotten that things closed down early in small towns. Hopefully she'd be able to grab at least enough groceries for her to be able to feed herself tonight before the place shut down entirely.

Making a mental note to do her shopping earlier in the day, she got out and began walking toward the store.

"You must be new in town," an older lady spoke, startling Hannah out of her thoughts.

"I am. I start my job at the clinic on Monday morning."

"Then you must be Hannah Reynolds. I remember you visiting your grandmother as a child. My daughter, Terry Landis, is the doctor at the clinic."

"Oh my goodness. It's a small world. I just got done talking to Terry a few minutes ago, and I got all the way home before I realized I should've made a stop at the grocery store."

"I'm eating at my daughter-in-law's house, or I would invite you over for supper." The woman stopped for a moment and then laughed. "I didn't introduce myself. I'm Marjorie McBride."

"I remember you. Your children are about the same age as I am, and yeah, I played with Terry when I was here over the summers."

"I'm so glad you're back," Marjorie said warmly, and Hannah had no doubt that she meant it. She felt like the woman truly remembered and was happy to see her, even if she did look tired and worn and perhaps was also in a bit of pain, to Hannah's medically trained eye.

"You know, you could come anyway. There's always room at our table for one more."

"Oh, I couldn't impose like that." Maybe if it had been Marjorie's house and not her daughter-in-law's, Hannah would've said yes. After all, she didn't relish going back to the house and eating by herself. She had never been much of an introvert. She loved spending time with people, and maybe that was part of the reason that she had wanted to be part of a big city hospital. There was always busyness and things to do.

"If you change your mind, I could give you the address so you can just stick it in your GPS." Marjorie started to pull her phone out of her purse.

"I couldn't impose like that, and plus, I'm a little bit tired. I've been traveling and then going over some things with Terry at the clinic."

"Of course. I'm always exhausted after driving for any distance too." Marjorie seemed to understand, or maybe she just wanted to ease Hannah's guilt at saying no.

"I'll take a rain check," Hannah said, hoping that Marjorie would invite her some other time.

"Of course. As I recall, you and your gram ate at our house multiple times when you were visiting."

"We did. I'd kind of forgotten about that until just now."

There were a lot of things that she'd forgotten about. Penny candy at Henderson's candy store, the Christmas festival that always seemed larger than life, and... Ben Tucker. Oh goodness, she'd totally forgotten about him and the massive crush she'd had on him every summer she'd gone to visit. Every summer she thought maybe that would be the summer he would notice her, but it had never happened.

Goodness, she'd forgotten about that.

Marjorie chatted a bit about how the kids had grown and a few things that had changed in the town, and then she said, "I'm sorry, but I really should run. They're going to be holding supper on me. Are you sure you don't want to come?"

"Not this time, but please ask again. I definitely want to get involved in the town."

"I understand," Marjorie said, patting her arm with her calloused fingers, which had obviously seen a good deal of work over her lifetime. "If you need any help settling in, be sure to let me know."

"I will," Hannah said, feeling almost as though Marjorie was taking care of her as she would take care of one of her own.

It was a good feeling. It also meant something to her that Marjorie and her gram had been friends.

Some of the jittery feeling in her stomach settled down. With talking to Terry Landis face-to-face, knowing that the doctor that she was going to be working with was a kind and decent person, and also having Marjorie reach out to her, she felt like maybe she had some friends in this town, and things wouldn't be as bad as what she had been afraid of.

Although there was still a part of her that just wanted to hide from humanity for a while and lick her wounds.

Knowing that was not possible, she finished her grocery shopping, stuck the bags in her car, and headed back to her grandmother's house.

No, she headed *home*.

Chapter Three

"I don't see why I have to get up at the butt crack of dawn," Mason muttered, throwing a disrespectful glance in Ben's direction.

Ben, off duty from his small-town sheriff position, pressed his lips together and tried to keep the anger from erupting inside of him.

"You can't lay in bed all day. It's one o'clock in the afternoon. I'm not asking for anything outrageously weird to have you up before noon."

"On a Saturday? There's no school. What do I have to be up for?"

"Why would you feel the need to sleep the day away? You went to bed at a decent time last night."

At least Ben had thought he had. But Ben had to admit, he hadn't checked on his fifteen-year-old son before he had gone to bed at midnight. And even at his age, thirty-five, which wasn't exceptionally old, although he didn't have the energy of youth, he had felt well rested by eight o'clock in the morning. Why did his son go to bed earlier and sleep later?

"You didn't tell me why it matters," Mason said, grabbing cereal from the cupboard and slamming a bowl down on the counter.

Ben bit off the words to tell him to stop slamming things around. He was already giving him a hard time for not getting up, and he'd mentioned that he needed to keep his room slightly neater. He didn't want to constantly pick at his son.

"I was hoping we could go fishing today. But at this rate, it's going to be dark before we get ready to leave."

"Fishing is stupid and boring," Mason spat his words, irritated and condescending, like Ben had suggested they go to McDonald's and play at the play place.

He didn't know how to reach his son. Hadn't for a while.

He bit his tongue again as Mason slopped wet cereal onto the counter as he dumped milk into his bowl, then Mason just left the entire mess as he grabbed the bowl and a spoon and walked into the living room to sit down in front of the TV.

He had already used the remote to turn the thing on before Ben found his tongue.

"We eat breakfast at the table," he said, feeling like all he'd done that entire morning was nag his son about all of the things he was doing wrong. And at the same time, he felt like he'd let a hundred things slide that should have been corrected. Where did he start? He wanted to have a relationship with his son, and he knew that wasn't going to be possible if all he did was complain about his behavior. Still, his behavior had been abhorrent, and there hadn't really been anything to praise.

"Are you serious? Why'd you wait until I sat down before you told me that? What's wrong with watching TV? It's better than just sitting down at the table across from you and feeling your condescension drip from every pore."

Mason made no move to either come back into the kitchen from the living room nor to turn off the TV set. In fact, Ben could've been wrong, but he was pretty sure Mason turned the TV up louder.

Some kind of weird music Ben didn't recognize thumped and pounded its way into his brain, making the headache that had been skirting around the edges of his temples start paining him in earnest.

He had moved in with his mother, who was at a ladies' aid meeting, and she would be upset at the mess in her house.

Not for the first time, he had to stop all the nasty thoughts that wanted to march through his mind over the way his ex-wife had acted.

Not only had she cheated on him, but when she divorced him, she'd demanded custody. He hadn't wanted to fight, but he'd also argued that Mason needed to be removed from the bad influences that he had fallen in with when he'd turned twelve.

His wife hadn't listened, and she'd insisted that not only did she get custody, but Ben had to stay in the same town and couldn't move away.

Thankfully, he'd been able to show the judge what a terrible idea that was, but not until Mason had turned fourteen and chosen to live with his mother.

He'd gone from bad to worse until Peyton, his ex, had said she couldn't handle him anymore. He was disrupting life with her live-in boyfriend, and they were expecting a child together, planning a wedding. She couldn't have an unruly teen who was in with the wrong crowd of people hanging out at her house. Of course, she blamed all of the kid's problems on Ben, saying that he hadn't spent enough time with his son since the divorce.

Funny, because he would've lived in the same house with his son if Peyton hadn't felt the need to cheat on him and then leave him and divorce him.

Ben failed to see how that was all his fault, but it didn't really make any difference. Mason had gotten caught in the crosshairs, and he was the one who had really suffered. Not that Ben hadn't suffered, because he had. Having a person's wife cheat on a man did something to his psyche that Ben almost thought was irreparable.

But as broken as he felt inside, he had to try to be the adult for his son.

He walked into the living room, grabbed the remote, and switched the TV off. Standing between the TV set and his son, he waited until his son looked out from underneath his brows, his mouth full of cereal, before he spoke.

"Go to the kitchen table."

He didn't raise his voice, but he used the tone that he would've used had he been on duty and needed someone he'd stopped for speeding to get out of their car. He wasn't asking. He was telling.

For a heartbeat and a half, he was afraid Mason wasn't going to listen. Honestly, he wasn't sure what he was going to do if Mason decided to defy him. At fifteen, Mason was almost as tall as he was, although Ben was heavier and definitely stronger still. Still, he didn't want to have to use brute force in order to get his son to listen. But he might have to use some tough love, and he wasn't sure exactly what all that entailed to get his son back on the straight and narrow.

Or at least headed in the direction of the straight and narrow, because from the road that Mason was on right now, the straight and narrow wasn't even visible.

After giving him a scowl, Mason yanked his bowl, spilling more milk and cereal, and stomped into the kitchen before slapping himself down on the chair and practically throwing his bowl on the table. Milk and cereal slopped out everywhere.

For the time being, Ben ignored the mess his son had made in three different spots so far in the last five minutes.

"This is how you pour cereal without spilling it," Ben said calmly, as he took the same cereal that his son had left open on the counter and poured it into his own bowl. "And if you don't fill it up too full, then it doesn't spill out."

"Like I care," Mason muttered.

"You should care, because now you have a mess to clean up in three different spots in my house, and if you had been more careful in how you handled your bowl and how you filled it up in the first place, you wouldn't have to waste your time on that, and you could get right to the other chores on your list."

"Chores? I have chores?" Mason asked, acting like the idea was preposterous. He huffed out a breath. "I should've known you just wanted a slave."

All right, Ben had to admit that he had to bite back a grin. A slave?

"If I were going to get a slave, they would be a lot more docile, and they wouldn't go around making messes that then I had to take the energy to try to then get them to clean up."

"Then why don't you just clean them up yourself? That would save you some time and energy, old man."

"My theoretical slave would also be slightly more respectful. They would not draw attention to my advanced years, but instead would regard my wisdom with awe and respect."

For the first time that morning, the scowl left Mason's face as he seemed to be trying to figure out what exactly Ben was saying. He could almost see the wheels turning in his son's head, trying to figure out how to turn that so it was somehow insulting him so that he could get offended over it and have some kind of flippant, arrogant, disrespectful comment.

It seemed to be too much for his adolescent brain, because he looked back down at his cereal bowl and stuffed another spoonful into his mouth.

"I guess that settles that," Ben said, not because he had to, but because the silence felt oppressive. "I did make a list for you, and I do want you to work while you're here. A house needs regular maintenance, and the people who live in it share the burden."

"I knew it. A slave. That's why I'm here. Shall I call you master?" Mason shoved another spoonful of cereal into his mouth.

Ben was kind of surprised at his lack of animosity towards his son. He definitely needed a good takedown, and he needed to have respect for his father, but this did not seem to be the time. Not when Ben was trying to develop a relationship with him. And on top of all of that, Ben knew that Mason knew that what he was doing was wrong.

It was true that Ben had worked while Mason was growing up,

but Mason had been a well-behaved and well-mannered young man until the divorce. Most likely his attitude was due to that and also to the fact that he had fallen in with the wrong group of people.

Hopefully this move to Mistletoe Meadows would change all of that.

Plus, Ben had enjoyed the time that he and his son had spent together, and he had a lot of good memories of the things that they had done. Sure, the divorce had marred some of those, and the fight that he and Peyton had had over custody, with Peyton eventually winning, had marred them as well.

Ben didn't know how to solve the divorce crisis. He didn't know how to make his wife want to keep her vows and to stay with the man that she'd married. Had he been such a terrible husband? Had she really needed to leave? Had she really needed to break up their family?

He didn't understand it. Didn't understand why Peyton's happiness was so much more important than Mason's childhood. But Peyton had assured him that it was. Or she would argue that it wasn't more important, but it was just as important, and that she wasn't really doing anything to Mason that hadn't happened to millions of other kids who had turned out just fine.

Ben wasn't entirely sure that they had turned out just fine, but he had yet to win an argument with Peyton, and he'd learned to just keep his mouth shut and let her yell at him for whatever she felt like. Which, when his mouth was closed, she was yelling at him because he wasn't talking to her, but when he opened it, she argued with everything he said. It was a no-win situation.

Maybe Mason felt slightly the same, although Ben couldn't really commiserate with him on that because he refused to talk badly about Peyton in front of his son.

"Mom is right. You're emotionally stunted and don't know how to relate to people. And you act like a child." Mason shoved back away from the table, set his bowl in the sink with a clatter, and started to walk out of the kitchen.

Ben supposed it shouldn't surprise him that his ex-wife had spoken badly about him and said those things.

"Come back here, Mason. I have your list."

Mason slowed, and Ben held his breath until he stopped, turned slowly, and walked slowly back.

"Yes, master?" Mason said sarcastically.

Ben pulled out his phone where he had written down the things that he wanted Mason to do, copied and pasted it in a message and clicked send.

"I just sent it to you. I don't want you to do anything else until those things are done. Once they are, we'll talk about going fishing."

"Maybe I don't want to," Mason said, but he didn't sound quite as belligerent as he had. Ben guessed Mason probably was desperate for love and attention and probably did feel like Ben had dropped the ball by letting Peyton take him. Or maybe Mason was upset that his mother had basically said that she didn't want him.

It was a complicated situation, and Ben supposed Peyton was right in a way. He didn't relate to people very well. That was why he went into law enforcement instead of some kind of teaching or counseling career.

"I'll be the first person to admit that I'm not perfect," he said, his voice low-pitched and devoid of anger.

"You can say that again," Mason said.

"I'm so glad I have a perfect son to use as my example so someday I can attain perfection just like him." Maybe Ben shouldn't be using sarcasm, but he couldn't help himself.

Mason rolled his eyes.

"How am I supposed to clean the gutters?"

"Do you see beside that line where it says I'm going to do that with you?"

Mason sighed, a drawn-out, imposed-upon sound that made it clear that having to work with Ben was akin to being on a chain gang. "Do I really have to work with you? It's going to take all day. You're slow and old."

"I think we've established the fact that I'm old. And I might be slow, but we'll get the job done right so we only have to do it once."

"Whatever," Mason muttered. "I'm going to my room. You can call me when you're ready."

"No, you can go out to the garage and get the ladder. I'll meet you out there as soon as I'm done eating. But before you do that, you can wipe up the messes that you've made on the kitchen counter, here on the table, and also on the coffee table."

Mason glared at him, but he went reluctantly to the sink, grabbed a wet rag, and cleaned up the messes.

Ben sighed inside. It was going to be a long day.

Chapter Four

Monday morning Hannah left her grandma's house in plenty of time to get to work at the clinic. It was her first day, and she didn't want to be late. But she had spent the entire weekend unloading and arranging her things, and also wanted to get to know the town a little. So, seeing she had an entire hour before she needed to be at the clinic, went into the town, parked, and strolled down Main Street.

It was quiet since it was early in the morning, but there was still a man in the window at the candy cane shop and another man making candles at the candle shop. She wanted to stop and watch but decided if she walked the whole way through town and had enough time, she might stop for a few minutes on the way back.

As she approached the town square, admiring the beauty and how neatly it was laid out, she noticed something weird on the gazebo in the middle of it. As she drew closer, she realized that graffiti must've been painted on the structure overnight, or sometime over the weekend, since it hadn't been there when she had admired it while making a grocery run on Friday.

The words were vile, and she cringed. Who would deface such a beautiful thing with such awful profanity?

She didn't really understand the mentality of people who enjoyed destroying things. She was a builder. She gravitated toward the good and the wholesome. A healer.

Deliberately defacing and destroying things was a mindset she didn't comprehend.

"Do you know anything about this?" a deep voice said from behind her, causing her to startle and turn, her hand going to her throat.

"No. Other than it wasn't like this on Friday when I came through town."

Her eyes narrowed. The man in the uniform looked familiar.

Could it be?

"Ben? Ben Tucker?" She couldn't keep the words from coming out of her mouth.

His eyes widened, and for just a fraction of a second, his sheriff-on-duty mask slipped from his face as his eyes swept over her as though trying to figure out who she was.

"I'm sorry. I don't recognize you."

Her stomach dropped. Of course he didn't. She was the one who had had a crush on him every summer she'd visited her grandma back years ago. He hadn't known she was alive then. And from the dismissive way he was looking at her, he didn't really care that she was alive now.

Shoving all of those feelings aside, she forced a friendly but reserved smile onto her face. "I'm Hannah Reynolds. I knew you when I visited Mistletoe Meadows in the summers back when we were children and recognized you from then."

There was no emotion on his face as he jerked his head, acknowledging her words but not showing in any way that her name was familiar to him or that he remembered her from their childhood.

"So you didn't have anything to do with this?" He nodded at the defaced gazebo.

Her eyes widened. He wasn't suspecting her of doing anything wrong, was he? Of course, he'd found her standing here looking at it.

"No. Of course not. You're certainly welcome to search my car or my person or my house. I don't even have paint. Or a hammer, or... anything that would've damaged the wood like that. At least not that I know of," she said.

She must've sounded sufficiently knowledgeable, because he grunted, wrote something down in the notebook he carried, and then turned back toward the gazebo.

"I just got the call not that long ago, and the person seemed to indicate that it probably happened overnight. Do you have an alibi?"

Did she have an alibi?

"I'm sorry, I live alone. But I guess if you need to ask me more questions, I'll be at the clinic today." She couldn't help it. Her words were frosty. Just because she was standing here looking at it didn't mean that she was involved in it in any way. Surely she didn't look like a criminal, did she?

Of course, probably he wasn't allowed to go by how someone actually looked.

"I'll take your name and number. If I have any more questions for you, I'll be in touch."

So he wasn't even going to let her escape with just a mention of her location.

Grinding her teeth and trying not to be unkind, she gave him her name and her number. There was no reason for her not to do it.

"I'll be mentioning that you were found on site when the officer arrived to investigate the crime."

"I just happened to be walking through. I had nothing to do with it." Now he was annoying her. Was this the way investigations usually went? Anyone who was found in the area was automatically a suspect? "Surely you have better skills than this. You don't need to go around accusing innocent people of heinous crimes just because they happen to be within ten feet of the structure when you arrive."

"You need to be respectful toward the police officer on scene,"

Ben murmured. But his tone was dismissive as he wrote in his notebook.

"Are you done with me?" she asked, wishing that she hadn't taken a walk through town to begin with. And annoyed with herself for recognizing him when he obviously didn't even know her. She was so pathetic.

She supposed she could have introduced herself as *Dr.* Hannah Reynolds, but she didn't like to do that. It felt a little bit like bragging and also like she was trying to use her earned title to command respect. She firmly believed that if she were to be respected and admired, it would be on the merits of what she had done, not because of a title she had.

Regardless, she had to put this behind her. She had a community who needed her and a new job that awaited, and she couldn't allow her irritation over an arrogant and incompetent policeman to derail her from the calling that she had, which was to help patients and heal them with God's help.

Because of the extra time she spent at the gazebo, she did not stop to watch the candles being made but instead drove straight to the clinic after she got to her car.

Unsurprisingly, Terry was already there.

"You're early," Terry said, looking up from an iPad with a smile.

"It wouldn't do to be late on my first day. Plus, I'd be lying if I said I wasn't eager to start."

And nervous. The last time she'd practiced medicine, she'd made a horrendous mistake. It had not cost anyone their life, and the stakes were not as high at the clinic as they were at the hospital. That didn't mean that she didn't have that in the back of her head and that it didn't make her feel insecure and like... maybe she didn't have what it took to be a doctor.

Not that her medical degree hadn't been fully and completely earned, because it had.

"Are you ready?" Terry asked, pushing herself up from where she had been sitting.

"Absolutely."

"All right then, I'll go over today's patients with you. We also take walk-ins as our schedule allows, and so this schedule might not be everyone we see. But at least I can give you a little bit of the background for these folks. I'm sure as you're here longer, you'll get to know folks on your own."

"I appreciate all the help I can get." Hannah was sincere about that. From her understanding, small towns were rather tight-knit, and it would help to have a little bit of information tucked in her back pocket so that... even if she didn't quite fit in, she knew a little something about the people she would be treating.

"Our first patient will be Mr. Jones. He's owned a farm in the area for more than fifty years. He bought it from his parents, who also bought it from their parents."

"In other words, his family farm has been in the area for generations."

"Exactly. He's a little crusty, but he's got a good heart. Still, he's not going to do any kind of newfangled medicine. So I've been trying to do a holistic approach while noting that he declines any kind of medication I suggest."

"I see. So that's the way you handle things?" She knew that if there were any kind of lawsuits, meticulous notes needed to be taken that proper care had been offered and suggested and then declined by the patient.

"Yes. I have not told anyone that they cannot continue to come if they don't abide by what the medical standards suggest. I just can't do that. Even though my insurance company has threatened to drop me over and over."

"I see."

Hannah shivered a bit. The idea of not having insurance was scary. Lawsuits could, and often did, run into the millions of dollars. They needed to be covered. Still, she truly believed from the depths of her soul that patients should have the final say in their care. Doctors were not infallible, and they certainly were not God. They could give recommendations, but she'd seen doctors give ultimatums and unceremoniously and rather rudely kick patients out of their practice for not doing exactly what they were told. She just didn't feel that was the right way to handle it either.

"The second patient will be my mother. She... she has an issue that no one in the family knows about." Terry looked up, and Hannah met her eyes. They both knew that as doctors, all medical information had to be kept confidential. But Terry was telling her that what would normally be casual conversation could not be.

"She has leukemia, and she has decided not to go with traditional treatment."

"Oh." Hannah didn't know what else to say. Leukemia was usually very easily treated in most cases. But with Marjorie choosing not to do treatment, she was setting herself up for a slow and possibly very painful death.

"How long has she refused treatment?"

"She was diagnosed about nine months ago, I believe. At first she didn't want to do any treatment at all, but I started researching natural treatment options, and... I'm kind of doing that on the side." She seemed a little sheepish about it, and Hannah understood why. Medical doctors did not practice alternative medicine. It could void their license, cause their insurance to cancel, and get them into a world of trouble.

"Because she's your mother?"

"Yes. I know she's not going to sue me, and she's not going to say anything either. But she does come here for blood tests and other things. And you're going to know about it."

"I see."

That was a hard one, but she understood. No one would want to see their mother at least not try to fight the cancer.

"Are the methods working?"

"I suppose. She's not gotten worse. But her recovery has been slow, if you can call it that. She's also very tired constantly. And... I'm just not sure if it's going to work or not."

Hannah nodded, and Terry seemed to gather herself.

"You might end up talking to her because I have Brenda Bryant scheduled at the same time, and she's already told me that she won't see anyone but me. I wouldn't mind if you have time to pop into the room to say hi. I suppose that will be the best way to ease you into these patients who refuse to broaden their horizons and see a different provider."

"All right. I'll make a note of doing that, and I can definitely see your mom. I met her on the street when I was going grocery shopping, and she's just as wonderful as I remember her." The idea that she had cancer was devastating. But it made sense because she had noticed that the woman seemed tired and worn.

"Yes. I tried to explain to Mom that she needed to take the treatments for the cancer because the town needed her, not just because I selfishly wanted her."

"She's definitely a wonderful woman. Why did she say she didn't want to take the treatments?" Hannah asked this, even though she knew she could look at the chart and the information was most likely there.

"I think she was afraid, honestly. But she also said she was ready to die. And if God wanted to take her, He could."

"So she doesn't believe in traditional medicine?" She thought that was odd, considering that Marjorie had a daughter who was a doctor.

"I don't think that's it necessarily. Although she definitely puts more faith and trust in God than she does in medicine." Terry gave a self-effacing smile, as though she knew it was odd considering that she was a doctor.

"I do too. At least I say I do. Although... I don't know if I had cancer that I would just calmly say I'll trust God to do whatever He wants. That's... that's a crazy amount of trust and faith. Because... she could die." She knew that Terry knew that, but sometimes saying the words out loud just made them more real.

"I know, right? But even if she did the traditional medicine, she could still die. Or, as she said to me, she could be hit by a car walking down the street. God could take her whenever He wants to. And... somehow she's not really afraid."

"But she's afraid of cancer treatment?"

Even as she asked that question, Hannah knew it was a legitimate fear. Sometimes the treatment was almost worse than the disease, and she knew people could die from the treatment rather than the disease. Or at least die as a consequence of taking the treatments. They could be really nasty and harsh, but they needed to be in order to fight the cancer.

"She just has such a calm peace about her, and I'm not saying that she's never scared. I have seen her afraid. And I know when she made this decision it was very difficult for her, because... who wants to die?" Terry huffed out a breath. "Although I think it's more that she just doesn't want the pain. And I promised her, as much as I was able, that if she chose to go the natural way, I would make sure that she did not end up in pain because of it."

"That's a pretty tall order."

"I know. She might not be conscious, but she won't feel pain. Not if I can help it."

It was easy to see that Terry was resolved about this. And Hannah appreciated the fact that as much as she could, she was going to allow her mother to make her own decisions about her treatment and the way she was going to die. Sometimes in Hannah's experience, the medical establishment could railroad a person and bully them into choosing what they thought was the best way rather than allowing a person the autonomy of making a choice that the doctor considered to be wrong. It was something she'd turned a blind eye to so far in her career, but Terry brought it out front and center and forced her to think about it. The thoughts weren't pleasant.

To Hannah's surprise, after the office staff came in and the nurse as well, Terry led them all in a prayer before the day started.

That was new. Of course, a lot of things were new. It was much, much different than the big city hospital she was used to.

Not worse, to her surprise. She thought the adjustment would be in the fact that the clinic didn't have as much medicine or access to care like the hospital did, and as the day went on, that was true. But the cases they couldn't handle were sent to a hospital that could, and those were few and far between. For the most part, they saw people needing stitches or people who were diagnosed with flu or ear infections, sinus infections, and those types of things.

Chapter Five

By the time it was time for her to see Marjorie, she wondered how Terry had managed to do everything by herself. Especially since, from what Hannah could see, Terry spent as much time with the patient as the patient felt like they needed.

That meant the waiting room was often full, and wait times were long.

"Hi Marjorie. I'm Hannah, Dr. Hannah Reynolds."

"I remember. We just met in the parking lot. Your grandmother and I were friends."

"Sometimes when people see me in the office setting, they don't recognize me. I think it's the white coat." She did wear a lab coat. It gave her a spot to keep all of the things she needed to carry around.

"Oh, I think I'd recognize your beautiful nut-brown eyes anywhere. You always had such a sparkle."

Marjorie didn't seem to be giving her a fluffy compliment but rather sincerely talking about something that she had observed. Her words made Hannah smile.

"Not too many people compliment me on my eyes. Thank you."

"I don't know why they wouldn't. They're definitely one of your most striking features."

"You seem to know just what to say," Hannah said, thinking about how being around Marjorie made her feel at ease.

"I feel like I never know what to say. I just say what I think and pray it's for the best."

"I have to really work on my thoughts. I could never say everything I think." And she supposed that was the way it was. Once a person got their thoughts under control, they could afford to say whatever came into their mind.

"I think it's just a matter of getting close to God. And that's by prayer and reading the Bible. We often think that we need to do something special, like a certain devotion book or worship services, or that there's some kind of Bible study book or Bible club, but it's really just you and God and God's Word. That's all it takes."

"You're right. That seems too simple." She knew it was true, but it did seem like it should be harder somehow. People always wanted to take the things of God and turn them into some kind of hard-to-do ritual. When in reality, salvation was simple: just repentance and then belief in Christ. So easy, and yet... humans wanted to make it into a works-based thing that gave them something to strive for.

"I think sometimes we feel like it should be hard because it's so big. After all, we're reconciled with God and saved from eternity in hell. It feels like we should be doing something big to achieve that."

"Exactly. We think we should go around working as hard as we can, doing good works and saying so many prayers or something. But that's not the way it works at all. And if we just take a few minutes to read the Bible, we'd understand that."

"It makes us feel better." She paused. "But there are people who go the other way too. Use belief in Christ as a get-out-of-hell-free card and then don't think about the fact that God commands us to be holy because He's holy, and that as Christians, we're held to a higher standard. An impossible standard, because we're supposed to be like Jesus."

"Yes, it's confusing, I suppose, where we get the idea that we have to work our way into heaven when nothing could be further from the truth. But because we're going to heaven and because we love God, we want to please Him with our lives. And in fact, the Bible says that our lives are a reasonable sacrifice. So we give that to God."

"And isn't that hard to do," Hannah said, thinking about how hard it was for her to give up her life. She had plans and dreams and things she wanted to accomplish. And then she hadn't been given a choice about what she was going to do.

"You've had trouble with that?" Marjorie asked gently.

"I suppose so. I suppose what happened that brought me here made me feel like everything I had worked for was going up in smoke."

"But at the end of the day, God knew, and God had to have orchestrated it, or at least allowed it."

"Exactly."

"I feel that way about my cancer. God allowed it. I'm not sure why, and I'm not sure if it's for me or someone else."

"Is that why you're not taking treatments?"

"I suppose I would take treatments if I really felt like God wanted me to, but I just didn't have a peace about it. And I was also scared to death to do it too." She laughed a little.

"So do you think that's why you didn't feel a peace about it?" Hannah had never been quite sure how she could tell whether it was God's will or her own will, her own desires, her own fear talking.

"I told God I would do whatever He wanted me to. And I just felt like the decisions that I made were the right ones. I suppose when I get to heaven, I'll know for sure. But sometimes I also think that God's fine with any decision that we make, you know? That He'll work it out for good, and as long as the decision isn't a moral one—like if I had to steal medicine in order to take the treatment, I would know that that was not the right decision to make, you know?"

Hannah laughed. "I know. That makes sense."

"Since it was just a matter of taking treatment, which was

morally okay, or not taking treatment, which was also morally okay, I felt like there might not have been a specific way I had to decide. You know?"

"That makes sense."

And it really did. That there were some decisions that either way would be fine. Whether that was true or not, whether it worked or not, Hannah couldn't say for sure. But she couldn't think of anything in the Bible that said that was wrong. Although she definitely thought it was always wise to ask for God's guidance and to do what a person thought the Lord wanted them to.

She had to admit that had not been the way she had lived her life. She hadn't prayed at all about what job to take. She'd taken the one that would be the most prestigious. After all, wasn't that why she became a doctor?

She questioned that though. Because she definitely could have a ministry here, looking at Marjorie, who had no medical degree of course, but served the town in a way that would be irreplaceable. That's what she wanted to do: be needed and be a blessing wherever she was.

She and Marjorie talked some more and went over the treatment Terry had given her. Although Marjorie was just in to have some blood drawn and tested.

She was on her way shortly, and as Hannah went to the nursing station to check on her notes, Cassie, the receptionist, asked her if she would be able to squeeze in some stitches.

"Of course." It had been a while since she'd done stitches, but she certainly knew how.

"All right. I already have them in exam room two. Michelle, the nurse, has already done the preliminaries, and we're just waiting for either you or Terry to stitch him up."

"All right. Are the sutures in there?" she asked, confirming with Cassie where everything was, since this was her first time doing stitches at the clinic.

Once she was confident she would have everything she needed, she walked back down the hall to exam room two and went in the back door.

She almost turned around and walked back out. Ben stood inside, with what looked like a deputy.

The deputy had bloody gauze pressed to his hand.

"Good afternoon, gentlemen," she said, getting a hold of herself. She could be professional. She was a professional.

"Hey, Doc," the deputy said.

She glanced at the chart. His name was Gordon.

"It looks like you stuck your hand somewhere you shouldn't have, Gordon," Hannah said, making conversation and noticing that Ben said nothing.

"Just doing what the boss told me to," Gordon said, glancing at Ben.

Ben raised his brows. "I did not tell you to touch that glass."

"No, but you did tell me to look behind the board that was there to see if there was any graffiti sprayed on the back of the gazebo. How was I to know there was broken glass back there?"

"Sometimes our eyes tell us things if we use them," Ben said, a note of irony in his voice.

"That's true, Ben," Hannah said, thinking about how he hadn't recognized her. She had been mulling that over, maybe not thinking about it directly, but realizing that she and Ben had had enough interactions when they were children that... surely he would've recognized her? She hadn't changed that much. Marjorie had recognized her right away.

And even if he hadn't recognized her looks, surely when she said her name... anyway, she needed to let it go.

"Let me see that," she said after she snapped a pair of latex gloves on her hands and held her hand out for Gordon's hand.

If Ben had a reaction to her words, he didn't let on. And she wasn't going to rub it in. So he didn't recognize her—that was fine. Didn't remember her either—that was fine as well.

"Were you looking at the graffiti on the gazebo?" she asked

casually as her eyes roved over the cut, figuring out exactly how she was going to stitch it. It seemed pretty straightforward, but it definitely was deep enough and big enough that it needed stitches.

"Yeah. Someone's been doing a rash of vandalism in town. Normally, we don't have to worry about it, do we, Boss?" Gordon said, glancing at Ben.

She took out her tools and began to stitch up Gordon's hand.

She wasn't sure whether that was to bring him into the conversation or whether he was trying to get Ben to talk. Whatever it was, Ben just shrugged his shoulder. "Whoever it is is getting away with it. As soon as they stop getting away with it, it will end. Once people see that we punish vandals, the vandalism will end. It's just a matter of catching them." His eyes narrowed at Hannah, as though he were still considering her a suspect.

"I can take pictures of my whereabouts and send them to you if you're concerned that I might be involved in this spree of vandalism. Although if it started before I moved to town on Friday, then you can cross me off your list of suspects."

"We're not suspecting you of anything," Gordon said, looking at Hannah like she'd lost her mind. "You're a doctor. You're not going to go around spray-painting profanity on town property." He huffed out a breath. "Plus, we've got surveillance video, and it looks like a teenage boy. No one thinks it's you." He repeated, just in case Hannah had any lingering doubts.

So Ben had surveillance video. Did he know that when he was accusing her earlier that day? Was he just giving her a hard time, or was he seriously just naturally suspicious of everyone? Surely he didn't go around accusing the townspeople of vandalizing their town without just cause?

Ben's eyes met hers for a second, and then his gaze slid away, as though he were guilty.

That's exactly what she thought. He'd just been giving her a hard time.

But why?

She didn't have an answer to that question, and she probably wasn't going to get one, so she snipped off the last suture, murmured a few words, then turned and walked out, leaving the door cracked just a little, as she walked to the computer and started typing some information in.

She didn't mean to eavesdrop, but the deputy's voice came from the open door.

"Do you think it was Mason?" he asked, as Hannah tried to figure out who in the world Mason was.

"I hope not."

The reply was short, but it had emotion in it that tugged at Hannah's heart, even though she didn't want it to. Obviously, whoever Mason was, Ben loved him.

"I hope not too," Gordon said, although his words seemed fatalistic, like he'd already reached the conclusion that it was Mason.

A police officer, along with the rest of America, was supposed to hold people innocent until they were proven guilty. But sometimes crimes were so obvious that it was hard not to come to that conclusion. It felt like common sense.

Who was Mason?

"I don't know what I'm going to do with that boy," Ben muttered. "The divorce did not help."

Could Mason be Ben's son?

"I know we always feel guilty about the things that happen to us and how they affect our children. But you can't help what your ex did. If she had been faithful, if she had kept her vows, if she had done what she was supposed to do, Mason probably would be the straight-A student he was before everything happened."

"I know. I just wish there was something I could do to get my son back."

So it was his son.

Hannah's eyes opened wide, and her fingers stilled on the keyboard. Ben's son was having issues?

It made her feel a lot more sympathetic to Ben's situation. How terrible would it be to be a sheriff in charge of keeping law and order in your jurisdiction and to have your own son be the top suspect in a vandalism crime? She couldn't even imagine how devastating it must be.

"I think I have everything entered," she spoke to Cassie as she finished up the information. "Would you mind taking a look at this?" It wasn't the first one that she'd done by herself, but it was still her first day, and she wanted to make sure she was doing everything correctly.

Cassie smiled, not seeming to be put out at all, as she pushed back away from her chair.

"Of course," she said, looking as cheerful and sunny as the bouquet of flowers on her desk.

It made Hannah wonder if Cassie had a boyfriend who sent her flowers or if she just decorated her own desk. She seemed like the kind of person who made things better and brighter wherever she went.

"It all looks good to me," Cassie said after checking the information on the screen. She straightened and added, "I know that you have patients waiting, but I just wanted to remind you of the town meeting for the annual Mistletoe Meadows community festival. I didn't know if you were going and wondered if you wanted to go with me?"

"I... I'd love to," Hannah said, caught a little off guard. She did want to get involved in the town and be a part of everything, like she'd mentioned to Terry. And she appreciated being invited, not once, but twice.

"Sweet. It's tonight at seven. Would you like to meet somewhere? Or I could pick you up?"

"If you don't mind, I could pick you up. I have to drive into town from my grandma's farmhouse anyway."

"Oh, that'll work. I just live right down the street, over top of the candle shop. I can be down on the sidewalk at five till?"

"Sure. Do we have to get there early to make sure we get a seat?"

"There's plenty of seating. Unless you wanted to sit in the front. Those seats usually go quickly. But you're also more likely to get volunteered for stuff." She laughed a little. "I like to volunteer, but I like to select my projects myself."

"I'm with you. I want to have a little say in what I do."

"In the back it is, then," Cassie said.

She walked back to her seat with a little spring in her step.

Hannah's lips curved up in a smile. It was nice to be welcomed into town and invited places. Maybe on some level she'd rather stay home and eat ice cream and read a book, but this was truly what she wanted: to be involved in the town.

It made her feel warm and happy. Even though she had to go face Ben again, she didn't mind. After all, he was fighting his own battles. And even though they would probably never get along, she could give him grace, if only in her mind. She would not envy his position as parent and sheriff with a troubled teen, and that alone made it a lot easier to be kind to him as she finished up the paperwork and sent the sheriff and his deputy on their way.

Chapter Six

"I don't understand why I have to come," Mason muttered as Ben and he walked into the town meeting for the annual Mistletoe Meadows festival planning. "It's not my fault you don't have any friends and can't get anyone else to go with you."

Ben tried to let Mason's angry words slide over him. It was true that he didn't have many friends in town. Sure, Gordon, his deputy, was one, and of course Ben lived with his mother, and he considered her a friend as well as his parent. But he definitely held himself back from getting too friendly with the locals, especially since he could only imagine how disappointed and upset they would be if his son ended up breaking into something in the town.

He didn't want them to think any less of him because of his son's behavior, but that was hard, since he thought less of himself. Like he hadn't been a good father. Or a good husband, since his wife hadn't wanted to stay.

He tried to shake those feelings off.

"If I felt like you could behave yourself while I was gone, I wouldn't have made you come."

Maybe that wasn't the best thing he could say, because his son's face hardened, and Mason gave him a look that was so withering that Ben almost flinched.

He loved the boy. Loved him with all of his heart and soul. But no matter how much he loved him, he couldn't make him do right or choose to live up to his potential.

Goodness, he didn't even care if the kid lived up to his potential. He just wanted him to not get arrested. The bar was so low.

"Grandma is saving us seats. Come on," Ben said once he found his mother, who had an empty seat on either side of her.

He took a chair on one side while Mason settled down on the other side of Brenda.

Everyone in town was there. At least it seemed like it, as Noah Parker, who owned the music shop in town, called the meeting to order.

As he did so, Ben noted that the new doctor, Hannah Reynolds, slid into the row in front of him, with the receptionist—he couldn't remember her name—sitting down beside her, smiling and giggling a bit before she quieted with the rest of the crowd.

He didn't know why his eyes were drawn to Hannah. She was nothing like his ex-wife, and he certainly wasn't looking for any kind of romantic entanglement. Of course, if he were, he would want the exact opposite of his ex, which was pretty much what Hannah was. Smart and studious, a bit quiet but serious and intelligent. She also exuded care and concern and competence.

Peyton, on the other hand, had been a whirl of romance, neither one of them doing what they had been brought up to do, but slightly wild and definitely reckless.

She'd been pregnant with Mason when they'd gotten married at the courthouse while he was on leave from the Air Force.

He'd finished his contract and then applied to the police academy. Those were rough years where they were separated more than not, but he thought they'd made it work. He'd tried hard, although Peyton didn't really seem to give him credit for it.

Regardless, things had settled down when he'd gotten a steady job as a state trooper, and he'd figured they were over the roughest patches of their relationship. He'd even suggested more children, which Peyton had been adamantly opposed to.

Maybe because she was already involved with someone else. The thought felt bitter in his mind, and he tried to focus on what Noah was saying.

"It's going to be much bigger this year than last. Last year we broke records. This year, we need to be a little bit more organized, and we're going to do a few new things. We're going to have a festival medical director, and we're also going to have a security coordinator. Security is not just for the protection of the people who are there but also to close down roads, direct traffic, and figure out what state permissions we need, if any. I'm not even sure how that works. So you're going to have to be able to work independently."

There was a murmur going through the crowd, and Ben was tempted to duck down in his seat. Maybe there was someone else who was an obvious shoo-in for that position, but he knew he didn't want it. He had enough on his plate, and if he were being perfectly honest, Mason was the one who was most likely to cause any disruptions to the festival.

He would do a better job of keeping an eye on Mason if he wasn't completely consumed with keeping everyone else safe.

"You should volunteer for that, honey," his mother said, leaning over and speaking into his ear while she tapped his leg with her hand.

"I have too many other things going on," he murmured back, although he knew he'd take the position if the town needed him to.

Noah continued speaking, saying that they were also going to have a director of music, and if no one else was interested, he would head up that committee.

No one else raised their hand, and Noah declared that that had been decided.

Unfortunately, no one else volunteered for any of the other positions, and soon Noah was calling names out of the crowd.

"Dr. Terry, I would volunteer you for the medical director. I know you'd do a great job. But I know that that's about the time your baby is due."

"It is. Although I'd love to do it. Maybe Dr. Hannah?" Terry said, looking back to where Dr. Hannah sat just in front of Ben.

Ben almost smiled as Hannah squirmed in her seat, almost as though she too were interested in ducking down out of sight. Sitting in the back the way she was, she obviously hadn't come expecting to be volunteered for anything.

"I could do that," she said, her voice sounding stronger and more confident than her position would've made Ben guess it would.

"That's great," Noah wrote down her name on the paper that was in front of him. "We'd like to have a tent set up where people can go if they have heat exhaustion, fatigue, and any kind of minor injuries, and have it stocked with first aid supplies. If you don't mind staying afterwards a little bit, I have a list of things that I was hoping you could include, and we'll go over that, along with all of the other heads of committees." He took a breath. "And if you'd like to have anyone serving alongside of you as a help, we'll talk about that then. And... you can either ask someone, or we'll have another meeting where we ask for volunteers."

Dr. Hannah nodded her head, and Cassie giggled and said something in her ear. It made Hannah smile as she looked at Cassie, and almost as though she could feel Ben's eyes on her, she looked around just a little more, and her eyes met his for just a second.

In that second, time seemed to slow down, and it felt like something passed between them. He wasn't even sure what. But it seemed strange, although not unpleasant.

And then it was over. Just like that. She turned back, and he ripped his eyes away, focusing instead on Noah, who stood at the front.

Although it took a few moments until he heard what Noah was saying, and his mom poked him in the ribs.

"Volunteer!" she hissed.

He wasn't even sure what she wanted him to volunteer for, so he kept his hand firmly down and stared at the podium, avoiding eye contact and hoping he could figure out from context what in the world was going on.

What had that been between Dr. Hannah and him? Had he been the only one to feel it?

He had to have been, and he tried to push it aside. He wasn't one for hocus-pocus feelings. He'd gone down that road once, swept away by youthful passions, and had married hastily. He certainly wasn't going to do that again.

"My son, Ben, is a perfect person for that, and I nominate him." His mother stood up and spoke, and he remembered just in time to keep his mouth closed, since it wanted to drop open in shock.

What had she volunteered him for?

Just as that thought went through his head, he realized that the seat beside his mother was empty.

Where was Mason?

"Ben? Is that okay with you?" Noah asked, and then after a small pause, he said, "Although if your mother says you should do it, I think you gotta listen to her." Laughter rippled throughout the crowd.

Ben grinned and tried to keep the concern off of his face. Where had his son gone?

"I'm definitely going to listen to her. What is that commandment about obeying your parents?" He huffed out a breath. "I don't think there's an end date on that."

He didn't think a grown adult was supposed to obey his parents, but they were definitely supposed to honor them. That was what the commandment said.

Still, following his comment, the crowd laughed again.

"All right then. You'll be co-chairs with Dr. Hannah on the combined committee of health and safety, as I just explained. Both of your committees are new, and we have no precedent."

Noah seemed to stare at him across the crowd. "You and Dr. Hannah know each other, correct?"

"Yes. We've met," Ben said immediately, to try to head off any weird introductions that would make everyone uncomfortable.

"All right. I'll need you up here at the front at the end of the meeting as well. We'll discuss whether or not you need any extra assistance and what that might look like."

Ben figured there were probably other things involved, such as what the budget was going to be and whether there even was one.

He wanted to sarcastically thank his mother, but honestly, he was happy to help out with his hometown. After being in the city for so long, he was grateful to be back and definitely wanted to do his part to keep things moving. He knew small towns didn't thrive on their own. It took people willing to head up committees and do a lot of work behind the scenes in order to bring in visitors and tourist dollars to keep the downtown businesses thriving and to keep the town bustling and healthy.

Without those people, the town would die.

Noah had started talking about something else when two things happened simultaneously. The first was that Ben remembered that Mason had disappeared. The second was the fire alarm went off.

"Is there a fire?" some woman said from near the front of the building.

After that, pandemonium broke out as a third of the crowd jumped up and tried to run for the door. There were too many people in the large community room for that many people to be able to make a break for the door. Several people got shoved aside, and it seemed like chaos for a while.

Ben noticed a lady to his left get knocked down, and whoever ran into her didn't even seem to notice as they continued to rush to the door.

As Ben stood, looking to see where the fire was, he noticed that Dr. Hannah had knelt down beside the lady while Cassie stood in front of her, blocking people from stepping on her.

Seeing that was taken care of, Ben continued to scan to see where the fire was. But he didn't even see smoke. Or smell it.

And then he noticed his son standing over by the fire alarm, a smirky grin on his face.

His heart sank. He should've known Mason would do something to retaliate for being forced to come. After Mason had been unable to provide any kind of solid alibi for that morning when he had asked whether or not he had vandalized the gazebo, Ben had felt like it was best to not leave his son alone.

The gazebo had been vandalized sometime between when Ben left the house and within an hour after he arrived on duty at the sheriff's office.

"It was a false alarm!" he called out in his loudest voice, even as he started to move through the crowd to reach his son.

Mason wasn't even trying to run, and Ben knew he would have to take his son in and file misdemeanor charges on him.

"I can handle this," Gordon said from beside him, glancing at Mason before looking back at Ben.

Ben knew that he should excuse himself, since he was too invested and would have a conflict of interest. After all, he didn't want his son to have this on his record, but there was no getting around it.

"I appreciate it," he said.

Gordon jerked his head and walked over to Mason, where they spoke quietly, before Gordon grabbed a hold of Mason's arm and led him outside.

In the meantime, Noah had regained control of the crowd again, and people had started making their way back to their seats. Ben walked to the back room and stood against the wall, his arms folded across his chest, and fought the urge to leave and go somewhere where he could hide. It was embarrassing to have his son create chaos. Although in all of the excitement, he wasn't sure if anyone had actually seen that it was his son who'd caused the problem. He owed Gordon for getting him out so quickly.

But he definitely couldn't expect anyone to keep this under their hat. The whole town was going to know. And if they were able to figure out for sure if Mason had been the one to deface the gazebo, that would be added to his list of sins.

"Sorry about the interruption, but I think we're done anyway. Thank you all. Sorry about the inconvenience," Noah said as he tapped the gavel and set the hammer down.

Ben glanced over to where his mother had been sitting. She was back in her place and seemed like she was just fine. At least she hadn't gone running for the door, and Ben had made sure she was okay before he'd walked away from her.

While he was looking that direction, his eyes caught on Dr. Hannah, who was also back at her seat, although the lady who had fallen was now sitting beside her. She appeared shaken but okay.

"If I said that you needed to meet with me after the meeting, please come to the front," Noah reminded everyone.

Ben gritted his teeth. He wasn't going to have any choice but to go up and do his duty, even though his heart was with his son and his mind was working on the problem of what to do. He really had no idea. Nothing in his life had prepared him for this. He felt totally inadequate to be a father, but it wasn't like it was a job he could quit. He had no choice but to continue on, no matter how terrible he thought he was doing.

With that thought in mind, he pushed off the wall and started toward the front.

Chapter Seven

"Are you sure you're okay, Mrs. Comerford?" Hannah asked as they all stood from their chairs. Hannah needed to get to the front, but she didn't want to leave Mrs. Comerford if she still needed help. The lady was elderly, and Hannah had been afraid the fall might've broken a hip. But after making sure that the woman was okay, they were able to help her up, and she seemed like she would be fine. Bruised, but okay. Thankfully, the lady wasn't taking blood thinners, and Hannah was not worried about internal bleeding. Blood clots were more of an issue, but Hannah had already talked to her about that.

"Thank you for your help. I think I'll be fine. I might be a little sore in the morning."

"I'm sure you'll probably be a little sore. Don't hesitate to call me if you need me, okay?" Hannah asked, waiting until the lady nodded gratefully and promised to do so, before she allowed her to walk toward the back of the building while Hannah turned and walked toward the front.

Maybe it was because of that weird moment when she'd made eye contact with Ben, but something had made her look at him once the pandemonium had broken out, and she had seen him looking over toward the fire alarm, and his eyes had been horrified.

That had made her glance over, and she'd seen the deputy sheriff apprehending a kid that looked very much like Ben.

As much as Hannah felt like she and Ben had personalities that would clash with each other, it made her feel bad for him all over again.

Even if the man wasn't the sheriff of Mistletoe Meadows, it would be difficult to have a son who seemed to be completely devoted to destroying his life and making his father miserable and embarrassing him at every opportunity.

"I'm so glad you were there to help Mrs. Comerford," Cassie spoke next to her shoulder.

"I appreciate you standing to make sure that we didn't get trampled while we did it. Although people were much more controlled than I expected. I thought there would be more panic. But after the initial rush, folks settled down."

"I think that's because there were several people with cool heads who were instructing people to calm down and file out in an orderly manner."

"Regardless, I appreciate you making sure that the crowd went around us."

"No problem," Cassie said with a smile. "If you need anyone on your committee, you know you can count on me. But for now, I need to run over and talk to Jane. She's starting a book club, and she asked me to co-chair it with her."

"Sure. This shouldn't take long, and I'll look for you when I'm done."

They parted ways, although Hannah honestly had no idea how long it was going to take. Hopefully she would be finished before Cassie, and Cassie wouldn't have to wait on her.

But she wasn't quite sure what she had gotten herself into. Still, she had wanted to help in the town, and she supposed this was one way to get started.

"I appreciate you both getting up here quickly," Noah said as Hannah made it to the podium.

She looked around to see who the second person was and realized that Ben had followed her up.

She nodded her head at him and smiled, although his face was serious, and he almost looked angry.

She bristled immediately at the look and then told herself to relax. It wasn't her, at least she didn't think it was. It was probably because he was worried about his son.

"Hey, I saw who pulled the alarm," Noah said softly, and maybe he had only intended for Ben to hear.

Ben glanced at Hannah before he jerked his head.

"I saw it too. I mean, I didn't see him actually pull it, but I saw a kid standing over there."

Ben jerked his head again.

"I just wanted you to know I'll be going to the station when we're done here, but we're not going to press charges. I know that you're working with him."

"It might be good if you do. As much as I hate to say that. There needs to be some consequences for his actions, and apparently the punishments that I've been dishing out have not been effective."

Obviously, it cost a lot to say that, and Hannah found herself tempted to put a hand on his shoulder or his arm to comfort him.

"Okay. I'll do what you think is best. I wouldn't want to be in your shoes, and I know that there are circumstances that... while maybe they don't excuse his behavior, they certainly explain it."

Hannah figured they were talking about the divorce and about whatever issues Ben had with his ex.

Ben nodded.

"All right. I don't want to go on about that, and there'll be more people coming up. But I wanted to talk to the two of you together. We can have two separate committees, but like I said in the meeting, I would prefer to put the two of you together into one safety committee and make you co-chairs of that. It would be more beneficial for the budget. That way we can allocate wherever the money needs to be allocated, since this is our first time and we're not sure exactly what we'll be getting into."

Hannah did not want to agree to that. She really didn't want to have anything to do with Ben. The two of them couldn't seem to get along, and he irritated her in ways she couldn't explain.

There was also that moment that they'd shared across the room, and she didn't want a repeat of that, whatever it was. Although she couldn't say it was an unpleasant experience.

"That's fine with me," she said, and hoped that she didn't wait too long. The men seemed to be looking at her and waiting for her to speak.

"That's fine with me too."

"All right. Then I'll let the two of you hash it out. If you need help, you can grab it from your friends, or you can let me know, and like I said in the meeting, we'll call a meeting and we'll get volunteers. If I get anyone who comes up and asks to help, I can assign them to your committee as well. We'll just have to play that by ear. I hope that we're not jumping ahead of ourselves and expecting the festival to be bigger this year than it was last, but that certainly seems to be the way things are shaping up."

"It's better to be prepared than to be overrun when the actual time comes."

"Thanks. I hope you don't mind going through a lot of extra work and aren't upset when the numbers aren't there." Noah seemed to appreciate Ben's words and seemed to be letting them both know that they could be doing a lot of work for nothing.

Hannah didn't mind. She agreed with Ben.

"That's how I feel as well," she said.

Noah nodded and then said, "I'll let the two of you hash it out, figure out a time to meet and that type of thing. I've got a few other people I need to talk to if that's okay."

"We've got it," Hannah said, lifting her brows at Ben, who

nodded. He seemed preoccupied, but that was to be expected after what had happened with his son.

Noah moved away to a few other people who had come up to the front to help out, leaving Hannah and Ben standing together awkwardly.

At least Hannah felt like it was awkward. Ben seemed perfectly at ease, other than the hard expression on his face and the obvious desire to be somewhere else.

So she figured she might as well take the bull by the horns.

"I feel like we didn't get off on the best foot, and I'm sorry. I'm really looking forward to doing my part to make the festival the best it can be. I owe a lot to Mistletoe Meadows and the small-town atmosphere." She thought about her own childhood and how the town had possibly saved her. Her grandma had a lot to do with that as well.

"Same."

She could've easily gone down the same path that Mason seemed to be headed down. In fact, she'd been on that path. Thankfully, people had intervened, people who cared. Like her grandmother.

There were times that she struggled to forgive her parents for what they had done, but in hindsight, she knew that what they'd done was in her best interest.

"Fair enough," Ben said, holding out his hand.

She looked at it for a moment, calloused and brown, before she took it in her own and met his eyes. She shook it.

"We have a few things we need to talk about, and the sheet that Noah gave us is something we should probably go over together," Ben began.

She nodded. "I can stay now, or we can set up a time to meet later?" She lifted her brows.

"I have a few things I'm going to need to see to, and I can't stick around."

She nodded and did not mention his son. Neither did he.

"Dr. Terry wants to keep the clinic open later in the evenings, and

I volunteered to take those shifts, so before noon would work best for me."

"I'm actually working morning shifts this week."

Their schedules couldn't be any less similar.

"I can take a lunch break at the diner though. It just opened in town. Maybe you've seen it?"

"Yeah. But I don't want you to have to give up your lunch break and—"

"I wouldn't be giving it up. I'd still be in uniform, and if any call came in, I'd have to leave immediately, but I stop in there to eat, and I can do that while on duty."

"All right. That sounds fine."

"Does Monday work?"

"It does."

He nodded. "Then we'll plan on it."

Chapter Eight

"Mason, do you want to talk to me about it?"

Ben stood at the sink, washing the supper dishes. It was a day after his son had pulled the fire alarm at the town meeting. Gordon had taken him to the station, but as promised, Noah had declined to press charges, so they hadn't booked him.

But Ben had promised that he would try to take care of the situation at home, and unfortunately, he had no idea how to do that. He wanted to take his handcuffs and handcuff his son to his right hand so they couldn't be out of each other's sight, but he hardly thought that would be an acceptable way to handle the situation for anyone in polite society.

Sometimes he wished he didn't live in polite society.

So he'd talked to Kate Wilson, who was the school counselor, and asked what she suggested.

She'd agreed that sometimes punishment was more effective than trying to talk things out, but she did suggest that he at least try to discuss things with his son. She had said that he might have some issues about the divorce or something else going on in his life. She had promised to try to talk to him at school, but she hadn't found anything out earlier in the day, because she had promised to call if she had.

Now that supper was over, during which Mason had not spoken a word, Ben figured the ball was in his court to try to initiate a conversation.

It used to be that he and his son had talked about everything and anything. In fact, when Mason was little, it was all Ben could do to get him to be quiet long enough for him to fall asleep at night.

They had laughed together often, and Ben had thought they'd had a great relationship.

Unfortunately, Peyton's cheating and betrayal had changed the dynamic of their family, and somewhere along the way, he'd lost his boy.

He had tried—they'd gone camping and had taken vacations together, but that had not helped anything. He'd had his son working in the yard with him, and when he'd finally gotten custody, he'd thought that maybe they could reestablish their old rapport. But that was totally gone, and anything that he suggested, Mason shut down.

"I asked you a question, son." He looked at his kid. Mason knew that if an adult asked a question, he was supposed to look them in the eye and give them an answer. He'd learned that from a young age.

"No." Mason didn't bother to look up from where he had a school book sitting on the table. But from where Ben stood, he could see he was just doodling on a piece of scrap paper and not actually doing algebra homework.

Ben wanted to rail at his son, but he made his voice come out modulated. "Is there something I can do to help?"

He didn't know what questions to ask. Didn't know where to put his finger on the problem.

"No. I don't need any help."

"Normal people don't pull the fire alarm at community meetings. That seems like a cry for help to me."

"Not me. I just thought it'd be fun." Mason didn't bother to look up, but there seemed to be a little smirk.

The smirk annoyed Ben, but he swallowed it down. He couldn't deal with his son out of anger or annoyance. He had to do it with love. Although sometimes love involved consequences.

Before he could say anything else, his phone rang. He dried his hands off on the dish rag and pulled it out of his pocket. His mother had gone to her ladies' aid society meeting, which was why Mason and he were eating supper by themselves. He was a little concerned that something might've happened and was relieved when a local number came up, but not one he recognized.

He answered. "Hello?"

"Hello, Ben. It's Roland McBride."

"Hey, Roland, what's up?" he asked easily, having known Roland since they were young but hadn't really fallen back into friendship since he'd come back to Mistletoe Meadows.

"Not a whole lot. I was wondering if you and your son might be interested in splitting some wood for a good cause?"

Roland had asked him to do things before, explaining that there was a secret network of people who, especially around the holidays, helped out their neighbors in need.

Ben didn't ask any questions, but he did pass along info to Roland when he got it. He didn't know if Roland spearheaded it or was just in charge of the outreach. He didn't ask questions.

"We'd love to. Where and when?"

"Tonight. It's a truckload of logs. It's been felled, but it needs split. It's sitting at the wide spot a mile outside of town."

"All right. We'll be on it," Ben said. "When does it need to be done by?"

"We have a week."

"All right."

He would try to get it done tonight, but it was always good to know exactly what his deadline was. He felt the thrill of excitement, plus that warm, satisfied feeling that came from knowing that he was doing something that would help someone else and be a blessing to them. It was too bad he couldn't get his son to feel that feeling. It really drove him to be better and to help more. But he supposed if his son didn't have it, there really wasn't a whole lot he could do other than pray that at some point it appeared.

He said a few more words to Roland and then swiped his phone off and shoved it back in his pocket.

"Hurry up with your homework, 'cause we've got some wood to split tonight." He turned back to the sink and started washing the dishes again. Unfortunately, his mother had never installed a dishwasher. Maybe that's something that he could take care of while he was living with her. Although if he had to guess, he'd say she probably would never use it. She didn't like the newfangled stuff.

"I'm not going."

"I didn't ask you. I told you." Sometimes he was trying to be both mother and father to his son, but he wasn't meant to be a woman. And while he believed there was a time and place to hold a child's heart, there was also a time and place for a dad to be a commander, the one in charge. To be masculine and to teach his son to be the same.

"And I told you—"

His hands stilled in the dishwater. This was a blatant disrespect that he couldn't allow to pass.

He turned around, praying that he would have wisdom to handle this situation correctly. His son was out of hand, and he didn't have any idea what he needed to do in order to get him back in hand.

"You know what you said was disrespectful, and I can't tolerate that in this house. You will respect your elders, especially your parents, your grandparent, and any other adult who walks through that door. That's just the way it is." He didn't allow any room for argument in his tone.

He didn't walk closer, but kept his eyes on his son while he spoke.

At first, Mason just sat there, and then he shoved away from the kitchen table, jumped to his feet, turned around, and punched the kitchen wall, putting his fist right through the drywall and screaming something unintelligible at the same time.

Ben was used to dealing with criminals and unexpected situations. Still, he blinked before he moved, striding across the kitchen and grabbing a hold of his son's free arm. His other hand was stuck in the drywall.

"That was uncalled for," Ben said low. Because just as quickly as the anger had burned in his son, it seemed to have deflated, and he just stood there, his hand stuck.

"There's a lot of things in life that are uncalled for, aren't there?" His son turned a hateful gaze toward him, and Ben's heart sank. His son hated him. It was obvious from the look on his face.

He met his eyes for a moment and then looked at his hand. The drywall had started to turn red.

"Let me get your hand out of there," he said. One emergency at a time. It looked like there was a good bit of blood coming out, and indeed, once he got his hand out of the drywall, he saw that there was a big gash on his wrist.

"We're going to the clinic." Was it still open? "This is going to need stitches." It was deep and already dripping blood on the floor. He grabbed some paper towels, folded them to make a small pad, and then held it to his son's wrist.

"Squeeze this."

Mason did as he was told. Maybe it was because of the sight of the blood, or maybe it was because he couldn't believe he had punched the wall. Ben wasn't sure, but whatever it was, Mason now followed him docilely out the door and got into the truck when Ben opened the door.

He would have sent a text to his mom to let her know that they wouldn't be there when she got home, but she didn't text, so he made a mental note to call her later. Feeling like a failure, he walked around the front of the truck, got in, turned the key, and pulled out of the drive, heading toward the clinic. He had no idea what to do with his son. And honestly, from his experience in law enforcement, he wasn't sure there was anything that could be done. Short of a miracle, he hadn't seen any kid who was as angry and bent on destruction as Mason was turn around and pull themselves out of the pit they'd dug. Most of the time, they went from juvenile offender to adult felon.

The thought made his blood run cold.

Chapter Nine

Hannah sat in the office chair, her hands going through some old files she had come upon. They had had a patient earlier in the day, Mr. Haywood, who had insisted that he had seen the doctor thirty years ago, and the doctor had prescribed for him to take iodine every day.

It seemed like an odd prescription, and Hannah was trying to find the old record, which had not been inputted into the new computer system that had been in place for almost a decade. Many of the people represented by the old files had passed away. They were in sore need of updating, as Dr. Terry freely admitted, but she had just been too busy to take the time. So she'd been doing what Hannah was now doing, which was going through the files when they needed them.

They were mostly in alphabetic order, but occasionally one was off, and Mr. Haywood's file had not been where it belonged. She was going through all the H files, just in case it had been misplaced.

She'd just found a file with the name Haywood on it and had pulled it out of the filing cabinet when there was a knock at the door.

Glancing at the clock, seeing that it was past 9:30 and they had closed an hour ago, she was tempted to just ignore it.

But that's not what a doctor at a small-town clinic did, so she pushed out of the chair and hurried to the door.

She opened it, not knowing what to expect, and was surprised to see Ben Tucker standing on the stoop, his son beside him, a bloody bandage pressed to his wrist.

"Oh my goodness, looks like you did a number on your hand. Come on in. I'm guessing you need some stitches." She opened the door wide so they could go in. "I'm Doctor Hannah, by the way."

"This is my son, Mason," Ben's introduction was short as he ushered his son in.

"Is it broken?" she asked belatedly, realizing that she wouldn't be able to take care of them if it was. Although she could probably find a brace that would keep his arm stable until they could make it to the bigger hospital down the mountain.

"I don't think so," Ben finally said, when Mason didn't say anything. "Honestly, I saw that it was bleeding and would need stitches, and just put him in the truck to bring him here. I didn't even check to see if it might be broken."

"What did you do?" she asked Mason, the way any concerned person would, but she actually had to put it in her notes. Still, it was nicer to frame it as a question that showed she cared rather than just gathering information.

There was silence.

"How did you do this?" she asked again, just in case Mason didn't hear her.

"Answer the doctor, Mason." Ben's voice was low, and it held a warning.

"I punched the kitchen wall." Mason sounded surly and annoyed. But he also, underneath all of that, had a note of insecurity or… desperation maybe. The kid was crying for help, Hannah would bet the farm on it, because she'd been there herself.

"All right. Come on into this room and let me take a look at it."

She led them into an exam room. Then she washed her hands with soap before putting on gloves. All the while, she asked questions.

"Why did you punch the wall?"

"Because I wanted to," Mason said. She was still facing the sink, so she didn't know if Ben gave him a look that said he had to answer or not. But it didn't sound like he wanted to.

"All right. That seems to be an odd impulse. Not one that I typically have anyway."

"Of course not. Because you're perfect."

"I didn't used to be. I guess I don't think I am now, either."

"Of course you are. You're a doctor."

Grabbing some gauze and some sterile solution, she walked over and sat down in the chair, scooting it closer to the exam table where Mason sat. As she examined his wrist, which did indeed need to be stitched, she spoke.

"When I was about your age, I certainly was far from perfect. I was angry because my mom had remarried after my dad died. It was barely a year. I felt like she was being selfish."

"Your dad was dead for less than a year?" Mason asked, his voice seeming to be interested despite himself.

"Yeah. My dad died in a car accident, and he left Mom with four kids. I never really thought about it at the time, but looking back, I'm sure my mom wondered how she was going to take care of us all. Maybe that had something to do with it, because the man she married was a bit older. He was kind, nice, but... I hated him because he took Mom's attention away from us, and I also felt like Mom was betraying Dad because she was with someone else."

"Yeah." That was all he said, but it was a telling word.

"So yeah, I started acting out, started doing some things I shouldn't have."

"Like what?"

"Well, I didn't pull any fire alarms," she said, lifting a brow at him. He had the grace to look abashed and wouldn't meet her eyes.

She looked back down at his wrist, continuing to clean around the wound so she could suture it without risk of infection.

"I skipped school some. I fell in with the wrong crowd. I went to some parties that I shouldn't have, and my parents—my mom and stepdad—were worried about me. So that year when school let out, my parents sent me to live with my grandmother."

"Where'd she live? Antarctica?"

Maybe he was being sarcastic, but she laughed. "Hardly. Although that probably would've been good for me too. Sometimes when you're struggling to survive, you forget the things you're angry about, and you develop a camaraderie with the people around you." She paused for a moment. He was probably too young to understand that. "But no, she lived here in Mistletoe Meadows. Where I live now, in the farmhouse."

"So you just moved in with her and stayed there?"

"No. I was just here for the summer. And then I liked it so much, I came the summer after that and the summer after that and the summer after that. And every summer until I graduated high school."

"So they thought they were punishing you, but it ended up being a reward." He was smart.

"No. It was hard at first. Grandma made me work. But I respected her. She was honest—not that my parents weren't—but she demanded a higher standard for me. She wanted me—expected me —to be a better person than what I was. It took a bit, but eventually I wanted to live up to what she thought of me. I didn't want to let her down. Because I knew she loved me. And she was making sacrifices in order for me to be able to have benefits that she didn't have growing up."

Mason didn't say anything, and Hannah focused on putting the Novocain in and numbing the area around the jagged cut.

Mason reminded her a lot of herself. Of course, he was a boy and she was not, but the signs were there.

Maybe there was something she could do to help.

Chapter Ten

Ben sat back, watching the interaction between Mason and Hannah.

He vaguely remembered Hannah being around during summers back when they were kids and teens, but he didn't realize why.

It was obvious Mason related to some of what Hannah was saying, and he kept his mouth closed, amazed that someone was actually reaching his son.

There was still a faint trail of guilt that it wasn't him.

But sometimes a parent could only do the best they could, and God sent someone else to help out.

Mason was actually giving responses that weren't sarcasm or belligerent, and Hannah acted like it was totally normal for her to be bandaging his hand he'd cut by punching the wall.

Maybe she did that all the time. Although it was obvious his son had a lot of suppressed anger. Probably because of the divorce, but he really didn't think that anger was focused on him, was it? Surely he was angry at Peyton for leaving the family and breaking it up. But maybe he blamed Ben for not trying harder or being a better husband, for not being able to keep his wife, although he had no idea how he would have been able to do that.

"All right. You're going to need to take it easy on that hand for a bit. In about ten days the stitches can come out."

"Should I bring him back here?"

Hannah started gathering up her tools. "You can. We can take them out. Or, honestly, stitches aren't hard to take out. You just need a pair of fingernail clippers. You clip them, and then make sure you get them all pulled out. If you leave a little piece in, you'll need to bring him back in, and we'll have to dig it out, and that won't be very pretty."

"That makes me feel like maybe we should bring him back in."

"We can do it, Dad. That actually sounds kind of fun."

Ben blinked at his son. He wanted to take his own stitches out? He couldn't even believe Hannah had suggested it.

"Didn't you hear her? If you miss a piece, she's basically going to have to do surgery on your wrist."

"But there's not too much of a chance of you missing a piece. It's all one piece of string, so you clip it, then just make sure you pull both ends out."

"That sounds really cool. I'm definitely doing that."

"Don't do it too soon. If you do it too soon, you're going to risk having it break open again, and it won't be as easy to sew shut the next time."

"Ten days, right?" Mason asked, and he seemed more interested and excited than Ben had seen him in a long time. Because of that, Ben pressed his lips together. If taking stitches out was going to keep his son out of trouble and grow a bond between them, then... he supposed he'd do it. Although he didn't think it was ever going to be part of his parenting toolkit.

"That's right. So get your phone out, look at what today is, and then count ten days from now and put a note on your calendar. That's when you're going to take them out. I'm going to grab you some waterproof bandages that you need to put over it while you're showering or any other time you might get it wet. Like if it's your night for the dishes."

"Dad and Grandma do the dishes," Mason said, and Hannah looked up in surprise.

"You don't have a night to do dishes? My goodness, you lead a privileged life." She laughed a little, and Mason shrugged.

"Dad doesn't make me, so I don't."

"Well, you should. Every kid should have to do dishes and cook and figure out other ways to help around the house. After all, someone has to do all that work." Hannah lifted her shoulder. "You don't want to have the adults around you always having to take care of you. Not at your age."

Mason seemed thoughtful, but he didn't say anything else.

Ben kept his mouth shut about that too. He just wanted to avoid the fight that he knew would ensue if he tried to get his kid to do more than what he already was. Plus, he had felt guilty because Mason's home had blown up. He also didn't want to listen to Mason complain more that he used him as a slave or anything of the sort. He supposed he had been letting his kid skate by in some areas, but Hannah was right. He shouldn't.

"Just don't get them wet. If you do, the stitches will disintegrate faster, and you might end up needing to come back in. So if you have any kind of redness or swelling or seepage, beyond a tiny little bit, come back and see me, okay?"

Mason nodded, and then Hannah turned her gaze to Ben. Ben tried not to flinch. There was that thing that happened when their eyes met. It was... not unpleasant, and at this point, he kind of expected it.

"I need to type up some instructions and do a little bit more paperwork. Give me ten minutes, okay?"

"Yeah. If you give me the bill, I can pay it."

"I think when we do after-hours work, it's on the house. But I definitely want to get you your instructions."

"I don't want—I didn't come in here for free medical care."

"I know." Hannah didn't say anything else as she disappeared out of the room. Ben felt a little frustrated and tried to relax the muscles in his neck by moving his head first one way then the other. She wasn't giving him charity—she was doing a favor. Maybe because he was a policeman. Or... he didn't know why else. But he wasn't going to argue about it. At least he was going to try not to.

"I wouldn't have thought that someone who was a doctor would've started out with the wrong friends," Mason said softly after she left.

"She got herself away from those friends, or she probably wouldn't have been a doctor."

"Her parents got her away from those friends."

Ben didn't say anything. That was part of the reason that he had moved out of the city. Mason had started hanging with the wrong crowd, and Peyton didn't feel the need to do anything about it. That's when Ben had started fighting for custody and trying to get his son away. He hoped he wasn't too late.

He and Mason sat there in silence until Hannah came back in with the instructions, went over them, and he tried to concentrate on what she was saying rather than the sweet berries-and-cream scent that drifted up from her general area.

It was a welcoming scent, and one he wanted to get closer to, to breathe more deeply.

An odd reaction, and one he felt like he was successful in hiding.

Still, when she put her hand on his arm after Mason walked out of the room, he tried not to show his shock and surprise. It wasn't that electricity flew up his arm exactly, it was just a—there was a magnetism there that made him want to step closer and put his arm around her.

She certainly didn't need his protection, so he wasn't sure where that urge came from, but he shoved that aside.

"If you need anything, if Mason needs anything, if there's anything I can do to help, let me know, okay?" She looked into his eyes, and her words were spoken sincerely. He found himself caught by her gaze, and his tongue felt stuck to the roof of his mouth, like he was sixteen instead of thirty-five.

He took a deep breath and tried again. "All right. I appreciate it." He wanted to tell her that she didn't need to bother to offer, and he wouldn't be taking her up on it, but at this point, he had no idea what to do to help his son, and he would appreciate anyone's help if it meant his son wasn't destined for a life of crime and incarceration.

"Thanks for opening the clinic for us. I'm sorry we came after hours."

"You can't help when things happen. I know Dr. Terry would like to be open all the time, but it just wouldn't pay to be open at night. Not in a small town."

"I'll try to make sure any injuries we incur upon our persons are during business hours next time," he said with a small smile, gratified to see her return it.

"Whenever it happens, don't be afraid to knock on my door, okay?"

"I appreciate it."

"Also," Hannah said as he started to move away.

He stopped and turned. "Yeah?"

"I'm staying on my grandma's old farm. I know you and your dad used to fish there, downstream a bit where the country club is now?"

"Yeah. They posted that about fifteen years ago, and only members are allowed along the banks now."

"Well, the river goes through the farm, and you're welcome to bring Mason and fish if you'd like."

"I'll keep that in mind next spring. Thanks."

"If you want to clear off any trees or anything, you can do that. Make yourself a spot."

He stood and stared at her. What was she saying? It took him a few moments, and then it hit him. She was giving him something to do with his son. Something the two of them could do together. A bonding activity. She wasn't pushing him into it or even making a suggestion. She was just offering, because living with his mom in town the way he was, he had no way of doing that himself.

He found himself nodding. "I think I'll do that. Thank you."

She gave a smile which showed her relief. Apparently, she had been concerned that he would take it the wrong way.

"I appreciate your interest and appreciate your offer."

"It's what I would want someone to do for me if I had a son like Mason. He's a smart kid," she added.

"Thanks."

Interesting. Most people saw the juvenile delinquent. The cop with the bad apple. The sheriff who couldn't control his own son. But not Hannah. She saw Mason's potential. And she reached out, offering what she had in order to help.

Of course, it was going to require time and effort on his part, but he was a dad. He would do anything to help.

"Have a good evening. I apologize again for the interruption."

"No apology necessary. That's what the clinic's for. That's what I went to school for. It was nice to use my degree instead of rooting through dusty old paperwork." She waved as he stepped out of the room, and he jerked his head in response.

Hannah was definitely different.

Chapter Eleven

"We've got an hour before we have to be at the top-secret security clearance meeting for the diplomat who's going to be making a campaign stop in our town." The police chief, Cade McLean, punched something into the iPad tablet he had in his hand. "You're going to need your badge to get in, so make sure you've got it with you, and be sure to pay attention. We told them that we won't need any help from the state, that our local guys can do it, and I want to make sure that we're not sloppy with anything."

"Yes, sir," Ben said, already having planned to attend the meeting, although it had been a rushed morning. After their late night getting the stitches in Mason's hand, their morning had been a little late, and Ben had had to shake Mason awake twice before he left for work.

The couple of times that Mason had missed the bus, Mason had called, and thankfully Ben's job was such that he could drive around and pick up his son and drop him off at the school.

Since Mason hadn't called that morning, Ben assumed that he'd made it out.

He felt a little bit guilty, which seemed to be his default emotion lately, that he wasn't there to get his kid on the bus every day. But Mason was certainly old enough to do a few things for himself. Maybe that's part of the reason why he hadn't had him doing too many chores either. After all, the kid got his own breakfast, cleaned up after himself, and got himself off to school. That should count for something, right?

Regardless, Ben continued to listen as the police chief spoke.

"We have some resources we can devote to the Mistletoe Festival. I understand you're in charge of the security committee."

"That's right."

"Well, you can let me know what you need, and I can let you know what we can provide, and hopefully they're pretty close. I think that there will be some officers who are willing to donate their time if we can't afford all the overtime pay."

"You can count me as one of those." Ben didn't necessarily want to work for no pay, but he was willing to do what he needed to in order to make the Mistletoe Meadows Christmas Festival a success. It brought in a lot of revenue for the shops in town, and he wanted to see everyone thrive, not just himself. Plus, everyone in the town was donating time. He could do that too. And security was his thing.

"You can count on me as well. Maybe someday we'll be big enough that we can afford triple time for officers who are working overtime during the festival, but right now, that's not happening." Cade lifted his shoulder. "With the new department store they're putting in at the edge of town and the revenue from that, things might just turn around a bit."

"I heard that they were using the extra taxes to fund local businesses. I take it that includes the police force?"

"To some extent, yes. The state has also stepped in and matched some funds. So we might not have to have as many fundraisers as we normally do. Things are definitely looking up for the economy around here."

Ben nodded. He was happy to hear it. Ever since he'd moved back, he'd settled in and felt more at home than he had in a long time. Although he regretted the demise of his marriage and knew that there were things that he could've done better, he'd been doing the best he could. Although that didn't mean that he couldn't keep trying to be a better person. He thought again about Hannah's offer to create a place along the river where he and Mason could fish in the spring. Honestly, he didn't even know if Mason liked fishing.

Yeah. Maybe he'd been brought down by the divorce too. Stabbed in the back and dealing with his own feelings of betrayal and not being good enough and trying to figure out what he had done wrong to cause his wife to need someone else. It was time he got past that, and he and Mason started building something of their own.

A family.

Maybe... he thought again of Hannah. Maybe that would mean it was time for him to start thinking about inviting another woman into his life.

The idea wasn't as unpleasant as he thought it would be. After all, after Peyton left, he'd kind of attributed her attributes to the entire gender, but that wasn't right. Hannah had already proven that she was different. Maybe... maybe she would be a good place to start.

He had to stop thinking about that and focus on his job; he brought himself back to the present just in time to see a slender figure walking along the road.

It looked like a teenage boy.

He squinted and looked closer. Was that Mason?

Yeah. That was definitely Mason. He slowed down and pulled off across the road.

He'd no sooner put the patrol car in park than his phone rang.

He grabbed it as he was getting out of the car. He really didn't have time to stop. He was supposed to go to that high-security meeting, but he needed to deal with his son, and when he saw it was the school calling, he answered it as he got out.

"Hello?" he asked, his syllables clipped. And then he put his hand over the speaker and yelled, "Mason. Stop!"

His son turned around, his eyes got big, and he looked both ways as though he were going to take off. Ben braced himself, because while he was a good bit older than his son, he was in pretty good physical shape, and he would at least give him a run for his money, although he had to tell himself that he could catch him if he needed to. The first step in accomplishing whatever it was he wanted to do was to have the confidence that he could do it. Even if he didn't think he could.

His son stopped, and the voice in his ear said, "Mr. Tucker. This is Henrietta Pliable, secretary at Mistletoe Meadows High School. I was calling to say that we've had several people stop in the office and say that your son arrived at school on the school bus and then walked off the property. I don't know if that's true or not. Was he supposed to be absent today?"

"No. He was supposed to be there. I'll get to the bottom of it and talk to someone in the office."

He wasn't going to say that his son was staring at him now, although he was. Ben had reached him and stopped right in front of him.

"That sounds good."

"Thanks," Ben said.

He swiped off and stared at his son.

"What's going on?" There was no anger in his voice, thankfully, although he felt it burning in his chest. Did his son understand that he was trying to do his job and be a father and a good citizen, and Mason was making his life exceptionally difficult?

But this wasn't about Ben. This was about Mason. He had to remember that. Because of Ben's bad choices, Mason's life had been exceptionally difficult.

"I'm skipping school. What does it look like?" Mason said with his typical sarcastic attitude.

"Get in the car," Ben said, turning and walking toward his patrol car. He'd forgotten until he was halfway there that he was headed toward the high-security meeting, and he wouldn't be able to take his son. What was he going to do?

He didn't quit walking toward the car and didn't turn around to see if Mason had followed. His son had darn well better follow, or there was going to be some severe consequences. The idea that his kid was supposed to go to school, knew it, and had chosen not to—although he probably should get some points for getting on the bus at least. And getting out of bed before that. If he were going to skip school, the smarter thing to have done would've been just to sleep in. Ben wouldn't have thought to look for him in his bed. Not until he'd gotten the call from the school, and now he wouldn't have had time.

He opened his car door and saw Mason walking around to the other side, and he couldn't deny the relief he felt in his chest. At least the kid listened, and he didn't have to have a confrontation right now.

But what was he going to do with him?

He got in and put the car in drive, pulling out on the road after checking for traffic.

"Aren't you going to yell at me?" Mason asked, slouching in the seat.

"Put your seatbelt on," Ben said, still whirling around in his mind, trying to figure out what to do.

As he came to the outskirts of Mistletoe Meadows, he saw the medical clinic sitting back, the parking lot half full.

Hannah had said that he could ask her for help anytime.

Was this anytime?

This was going to be a big ask. But maybe he could sit in the office, at least until Ben was done with the meeting and could figure out what he was going to do. Of course he could take Ben back to school, but how was he to keep him from walking off again?

He put the turn signal on and pulled into the parking lot.

"What are you doing?" Mason asked. Apparently he hadn't expected to stop at the medical center.

"I could ask you that."

"I told you I was skipping school," Mason said with a laugh.

"And you knew I meant why are you doing that."

"I felt like it." Mason clicked his seatbelt and yanked on the door handle.

Ben didn't have time to grill him.

He got out of the car and told Mason to follow him.

Pulling open the door, he allowed Mason to walk in before he did.

He hadn't expected it, but Hannah happened to be out in the waiting room, talking to a family, holding her iPad with her blood pressure cuff poking out of her white lab coat pocket and her stethoscope hanging from her neck.

She looked like a doctor this morning, when she hadn't last night. She'd looked like a beautiful woman last night.

Ben closed his eyes and gathered his thoughts.

When he opened them, Hannah had looked up, surprise lifting her brows.

"I don't see any bloody bandages," she said, tilting her head to the side, questions in her eyes.

"Can I talk to you for a moment in private?" he asked, not bothering to greet her.

She must've caught something in his tone, because she tilted her head and nodded, before murmuring, "Excuse me," to the person she'd been talking to.

Ben nodded at Mr. Greenwald and his wife before following Hannah to the back.

She opened the door, and he grabbed it and held it for her to walk through and then Mason as well.

Once she got back, she turned around, glancing at Dr. Terry, who stood in front of one of the closed doors, reading a chart.

"Do I need to wait for Dr. Terry to leave?" Hannah asked as she stood beside the counter, her hands at her side.

"No. I suppose not. I can't keep this a secret forever, I guess."

"What's wrong?" she asked, glancing again at Dr. Terry, who lifted her eyes and watched the proceedings but didn't say anything.

"Mason skipped school today. I have a meeting I need to be at, and I'm going to be late. I don't have time to take him back and deal with it. I... I was going to ask if he could stay here, but it's a terrible idea. I'm sorry." He started to turn away. What had he been thinking? She was trying to work. She didn't have time to babysit his teenager.

"No, it's fine. He can stay here. I mean, obviously we're limited in what we can do, but he can stay."

She didn't have to say that if he tried to leave, she wasn't going to be able to stop him. He was still bigger than his son, but Hannah was not.

"I wouldn't expect you to do anything extra or extraordinary. I just wanted him to sit here and not move until I get back. I'll deal with him from there."

"All right. I'm sure that'll be fine, right, Terry?" She glanced across the room at Dr. Terry, who nodded.

"Of course. He's more than welcome to stay. I think we can probably put him to work actually." She grinned, while Mason rolled his eyes, and then she opened the door to the exam room and disappeared inside.

"Go ahead. Put him to work. I haven't figured out what I'm going to do, but I'll have a plan by the time I get back."

"All right. That sounds fine," Hannah said. Then she grabbed a pen and a notepad that was sitting on the counter. "Do you mind giving me your number in case anything happens?"

"Of course not." He rattled it off to her, and she scribbled it down. Then he saw her write his name underneath it and underline it.

There was something about seeing her write his name. He wasn't sure why, but it sent an odd feeling seeping down his backbone.

"I really need to leave. I'm sorry to saddle you with this."

"You're not saddling me with anything. I noticed yesterday that Mason seemed to have an affinity for medical things. This might be a good opportunity to try it out. And you heard Dr. Terry. She's fine with it. You go on. We've got this, don't we, Mason?"

Mason looked surprised, and then he nodded.

"I'll stay," he said.

Mason leaving was what Ben had been afraid of, and the assurance that he was going to stay was what he needed to hear.

"I'll be back as soon as I'm done," Ben promised, and then he hurried off. He'd taken a job in a smaller town hoping for less hours, knowing he needed to try to figure out a way to piece his family back together—to piece the relationship between him and his son back together. He really needed to get on that. Or he was afraid that he was going to lose him completely.

Chapter Twelve

*H*annah watched as Ben left. There was a part of her that admired his long-legged stride, the confident way he moved, and yeah, a bit of arrogance. And despite herself, she found herself drawn to it. He was definitely a masculine man, and it almost was painful to see him out of his element, unable to deal with his teenage son, especially since it was so obvious that he loved him with all of his heart and soul.

"Hey, Mason. I was just about ready to go into an exam room and put some stitches in. You're a bit of an expert at this. I'll have to get permission, but if I do, would you like to join me?"

Mason turned and his eyebrows went way up. He probably had expected her to chain him to a desk somewhere, which honestly was her first thought. But there was something about the way he had been interested in taking his own stitches out last night that made her think that perhaps he had a natural bent toward medicine.

"Really? I could go in with you?"

"And help."

His eyes brightened. Just as she thought. He really was interested.

"Yeah. I'd do that."

"All right. Give me a second to check. I'm going to call you my assistant, and I'm going to say you're shadowing me because you're interested in a career in medicine. Would that be a lie?" she asked, not wanting to tell her patients untruths.

"No. I definitely am interested. I don't know if I'm smart enough to be a doctor though."

"It's not necessarily a matter of being smart enough. It's honestly just a matter of how hard you are willing to work and how much you're willing to sacrifice." She lifted her shoulder. "I'm not any smarter than your average bear."

That made him laugh, and she turned around and walked into the waiting room where Karen Hutchison sat with her son, Buster, who had wrecked his bike and needed stitches just above his eye.

"Mrs. Hutchison, I have an assistant who has joined the practice, and he's shadowing me because of an interest in a career in medicine. Do you mind if he comes in and observes and possibly helps by handing me tools and equipment?"

"No. That's fine," she said, looking up from where she had been trying to distract her son by using her phone.

Poor little Buster, at only eight years old, was scared and looked up with frightened eyes.

She smiled at him reassuringly.

"All right. We'll be right in then."

She nodded and then pointed to something on the screen as Hannah turned and walked back through the heavy door.

She closed it behind her, waiting until it clicked before she said, "That's fine with her. When we walk in, you need to wash your hands, and I'll give you a pair of gloves." She glanced at his hands. "I think you're going to need extra large." He grinned, and she lifted her brows. "Any questions?"

"I don't know what to do."

"That's fine. Just do what I tell you to do. The most important thing is to cause no harm. So we want to keep our hands washed, gloves on, and not do anything that's going to make it worse by introducing germs or causing an infection."

"Got it."

"It's also for our protection. You've got that healing cut on your hand, and if you get any of Buster's blood on you and it turns out he has some kind of blood-borne illness, like hepatitis or AIDS, you could come down with it. So your gloves are to protect you both."

"I understand."

He reminded her so much of Ben, the way he walked, the way he talked. It was obvious they were father and son, and Hannah hid her smile. Mason probably would not appreciate being told that he was the spitting image of his dad. Not right now anyway.

Mason did exactly as he was told, going to the sink behind her and using soap to wash his hands after she was finished.

She dug out a pair of extra-large gloves for him, and he put them on as she had instructed.

He seemed interested the entire time as they administered the Novocain, made a little small talk while they waited for it to take effect, and then began to stitch Buster's eye. She explained that she was stitching some of the inner membranes together first using a suture that would dissolve without having to be taken out.

That made Mason grin, and they shared a smile, remembering how he had said he wanted to take his own stitches out.

She explained what she was doing as she was doing it, and to her surprise, Mason seemed interested in the entire thing.

After they were done, she explained that medicine was not just about healing but also about having a conversation with the patient, passing the time, getting information by asking casual questions, and paying attention to the cues that they gave off.

That was something she hadn't expected in medicine. She'd thought she'd just be doing the straight-up administering, using her skills to save lives, but it was so much more than that, because humans weren't just bodies. They were souls and spirits too.

Mason followed her as she went to two other exam rooms, one containing a little girl who had strep throat.

She was able to use the tongue depressor and show the telltale white spots to Mason.

The next was for a toddler who had an ear infection. Mason seemed fascinated as she held the scope and allowed him to view the red and inflamed eardrum.

She put it in the other ear and showed him the healthy one, with the mother's permission, of course.

After that, her phone buzzed with a text.

I got called out to an accident on the interstate. Is Mason okay? Or do I need to figure out how to take him off your hands?

She glanced at Mason.

"It's your dad. He's being called out to an accident. Are you okay?"

"I'm more than okay. I don't ever want to leave here."

She grinned. "Maybe I can arrange that. Perhaps not the ever part, but if you're serious, I might be able to figure something out."

"Figure something out?"

She gave him a grin and then sent a text to Ben.

Mason is fine. Would you be okay if I called the school to see if he could do an apprenticeship here?

The answer came back immediately.

Are you serious?

I am. He's a natural, and he loves it.

Heck yeah. I can call.

You'll probably have to too. But you do the accident now, and I'll get the ball rolling at the school. You can pick it up when you have time.

Thanks.

His reply was short, but she had no doubt it was heartfelt.

"I have a couple of phone calls to make, so I'm going to see if Dr. Terry is okay with you shadowing her while I do that, okay?" She lifted her brows at Mason, who had been quiet through her text exchange.

"Sure." He shrugged his shoulder, like it didn't matter who he was with, as long as he was in the thick of the whole medical stuff.

As she suspected, Dr. Terry was perfectly fine having Mason tag along.

Hannah was thankful that Tuesdays were their busy mornings where they took appointments and walk-ins, and she had been on duty today. If she hadn't been, she wondered what in the world Ben would've done.

Chapter Thirteen

en walked into the community building for his first meeting with Hannah, unsure of what to expect.

He'd given the clinic a check for Mason, of course, but he felt bad because Hannah wasn't supposed to be on duty. She wasn't getting paid to treat him. Still, he couldn't deny that he was appreciative of the care she'd given, but even more so, she'd been able to connect with Mason in a way that so many people hadn't since they'd moved here.

Then, he'd dropped Mason off and Hannah had taken him under her wing and started the ball rolling for a work-study credit class with the school. He owed her. And admired her.

He hadn't considered allowing Mason to be out of school on a work-study program. Not until Hannah had suggested it.

"It looks like you beat me," Hannah said from behind him, causing him to turn around.

"I didn't realize it was a race."

She lifted her shoulder. "It's not. I just... usually, I'm the first person anywhere. It's an odd quirk I have where if I'm not a half an hour early, I feel like I'm late."

He smiled and nodded. That suited her Type A personality. The personality that surely drove her to become a doctor.

"I have a tendency to be early as well." He paused and then closed his mouth. He'd almost said that that was one of the things he and his ex had always disagreed on. He believed being early was a sign of respect to whoever the person was meeting. She was perpetually late for everything, and he felt like it was disrespectful. She felt like there wasn't anything wrong with it, although she couldn't justify or even excuse the habit.

"I guess since we're both here, we can get started early," she said, smiling as she set a bag down on the table.

"Looks like you brought things to take notes with," he said, wondering if he should've brought something. His hands were empty. He hadn't even brought a pen.

"I have a tendency to not remember things unless I write them down."

"I see. Before we get started, I did want to thank you for what you did the other night with Mason."

She waved a hand in the air, as he figured she would. "It's no big deal. That's my job."

"It's not your job that late at night. You saved us a two-hour trip down the mountain. And it's more than what you did stitching him up."

She pulled things out of the bag and brushed off his comment. But he didn't want to let it go.

"Since we've moved here, Mason has struggled. Actually, he was struggling far before we moved. And I hadn't considered giving him some kind of interest like that. I've talked with the school, and at first, they were reluctant to allow him to change his schedule."

"When I spoke with them, they said they didn't reward bad behavior with perks that not every student got." She rolled her eyes and lifted her chin. "But I told them that he had a knack and a gift for medicine, and it wasn't up to them to dictate or keep someone from their calling."

His brows lifted. So that's what had happened. "I wondered what caused it to change from my first phone call to my second. Because after the first, I got the impression that they were not going to allow it, and then something shifted. It must've been you." He owed her far more than he had even realized.

She waved it off again. "It's not a big deal. Mason was born to practice medicine."

"I love the way you see that in him. Most people just see a kid who's bent on getting in trouble." He was talking about himself there too. Because that's exactly how he'd been seeing his son lately. As someone who wasn't interested in anything but causing problems. When had he lost that vision? He wasn't sure, but he knew that he owed Hannah for giving it back to him. And for seeing the potential rather than focusing on Mason's faults.

"When I look at someone, I try to see the good. After all, I don't want someone to look at me and just see my faults. I don't want them to see all the problems and all my flaws. Because there are a lot of them."

"I don't know about that," he said, even though he knew he was kind of arguing with her.

"Trust me. They're there. But isn't that what we usually focus on? The problems? I do that in medicine all the time. I look at someone, and I'm looking at whatever health issue they have. That's the biggest thing. And I forget to look at them and see that they're a mostly healthy person. We're just trained to see the faults. The flaws. The problems."

"But you don't."

"I had to realize that was what I was doing. I suppose a school teacher needs to do the same thing. After all, she spends her day correcting the kids who are wrong and disciplining the children who don't behave in class. We forget to focus on the good. But that's what the Bible tells us to do."

"It's always amazing to me how the Bible has the recipe for a happy life, but we've glossed over it over the years and thought that we need to go somewhere else for our mental health, for psychology or whatever, when the answer is right there in scripture. Focus on the good."

"'Whatsoever things are lovely, whatsoever things are pure, whatsoever things are of good report,'" she quoted.

He finished the verse for her. "'If there be any virtue, and if there be any praise, think on these things.'"

They stopped for a moment and smiled at each other.

"It's all there."

There was something going on between them. He felt it. At least for him. Maybe not for her. And he wasn't sure he wanted that. He was already having enough trouble with Mason after the divorce. He didn't want to go through that again. But at the same time, he felt a connection, some kind of thing with Hannah that he hadn't felt with anyone else. She seemed to see him in a way that no one else did. Maybe that was because of her tendency to focus on the good.

"So that's how you did it? You just realized you weren't and made sure you started to?"

"It's not easy to change your thinking. But yeah, I knew that that was what I was doing, constantly focusing on the negative, and that's not good for your mental health, and it's not good for the people around you either. So I stopped. Little by little, piece by piece, which is also in the Bible. 'Line upon line.'"

"'Precept upon precept, here a little, there a little,'" he finished.

He liked the way they said verses together. Both of them knowing the same ones. That was something else he didn't share with anyone else.

It felt like there was something in the air between them, and he wanted to ask if it was just him or if she felt it too.

Instead, words he hadn't even been thinking about came out of his mouth.

"I remember you from when we were kids."

"Really? I didn't think you did."

"Yeah. You were always pretty studious, sitting around with your nose in a book or a notepad and pen," he said with a glance at the notebook that she had taken out of the bag and set on the table. A ghost of a smile swept over her mouth, but she still hung on his words. "You were always with your grandma too. And I got the impression that you were one of those goody-two-shoes, teacher's pet kind of things that if we were in school together, I would be the bad boy in the corner, and you would've been the goody-goody sitting in the front and getting A's."

Her brows lifted. "I had no idea you saw me like that."

He lifted his shoulder. He hadn't meant for any of those words to come out. He wasn't sure why they did, other than that was the connection that he felt with her. That he had known her for years, even if they had never really talked.

"I didn't know you even noticed me. You were so busy with your cheerleader girlfriend and all of your other friends that I can't believe you even remember."

He remembered. He remembered her honey-blonde hair, pulled back away from her face, falling in curls down her back, her dreamy eyes behind her glasses, and the way he'd thought that she was way too good for him. So he hadn't even paid attention to her.

He supposed he was right. Here he was, a sheriff in a small town with a troubled son, while she had gone on to become a doctor.

"Why are you practicing in our small town? You wanted to come back?"

Clouds covered her face, and the smile that had been hovering around her lips completely faded. She looked down.

"No."

The word was so soft he barely heard it.

Obviously, he'd stumbled on something that she didn't want to share and he remembered what she'd told Mason about her own troubled childhood.

"Never mind. You don't have to answer that."

She paused for a moment, with her head down, as though thinking about it.

Then she lifted her eyes to his, and he understood that maybe she understood about the pain that Mason was going through because she had some of her own.

"It's just fresh, that's all. Probably more fresh than it should be, considering that it's been more than a month."

"That's not very long in the grand scheme of things. It took me a lot longer than that to get over my divorce. Sometimes I wonder if I'm actually over it."

"Because you're still in love with your ex?" she asked, and there didn't seem to be any jealousy there, although he wouldn't expect there to be.

He shook his head immediately. "No. She was a mistake I shouldn't have made to begin with. But I would've made the marriage work, because that's what I do. That's the right thing to do. When you make vows and pledge your life to someone, you don't quit just because you realize that the person you chose was not a good choice." He lifted his shoulder. "It's just when you start to build a life with someone and they basically destroy it before they walk out —or maybe their walking out destroys it, I'm not sure—it just... there's pain there where there didn't used to be."

"I see." She nodded. "It's kind of the same with me. I made a mistake. It wasn't anything life or death, but it could've been. And I was terminated immediately. I wasn't given a second chance, and I wasn't given an opportunity to make it right. Everything that I had been working for was gone in that instant." She pressed her lips together. "I can understand it. Doctors can't afford to make mistakes. People can die when doctors make mistakes. But it was just hard, that's all."

"I bet."

"But I've come to understand that sometimes when things happen that you wish hadn't, that you weren't expecting, or things that turn your entire life around, like a divorce or something of the sort, God's in it. He really is." She touched the notebook on the table, and her finger slowly traced the spiral rings along the side. "Coming back to Mistletoe Meadows has been so good for me. I hadn't realized how much of myself I had lost in my pursuit of a medical degree and then in my pursuit of medical prestige. I had everything I wanted all laid out, and I'm just not sure that—in fact, I know that it wouldn't have been the best thing for me to do. Not even a little bit. I'm so glad it happened. It still hurts a bit. I'm not saying that it doesn't, but the change was good for me. And God knew it all along."

He nodded. He could see what she was saying. His divorce had been a shock, and like he had said, his entire world had crumbled to the ground, but it absolutely had been good for him.

"I can see what you're saying about me. It's true. I would've stayed with her until I died, but it probably wouldn't have been a good thing. Coming back to Mistletoe Meadows was definitely a nice benefit of that, but I'm not sure that it's been the best thing for Mason. He's struggling." He shoved his hands in his pockets and resisted the urge to pace. "I know eventually it could be the best thing that ever happened to us, but he has to choose to make it that."

"I think he's found something that he's interested in. I definitely think he's found something that he's good at. Whether or not he sticks with it for the rest of his life... I don't want him to feel like he has to. But I think he needed an outlet, and this could be it."

"I've noticed a change in him in the last few days, and you've been instrumental in that, I know. We've been at the river a few times too."

"I've heard you down there running a chainsaw or something."

"Yeah. There's a bunch of firewood to cut up. I figured I'd bring it up and stack it by your door, if you want it. I just hadn't gotten around to offering it." He'd totally forgotten all about it. Every time he saw her, he thought about the connection they had, something he really felt was attraction between them. When he was with her, firewood was the furthest thing from his mind.

"The idea of a fire in the fireplace is really sweet, but I'm probably not going to do that myself. So if you can find someone who could use it, go ahead and give it to them."

He nodded. It was on the tip of his tongue to offer to make her a fire, but that seemed a little intimate and like he was inviting himself into her house.

Plus, he understood what she was saying. A fire was better if it was shared.

"All right. Thanks." It sounded like she had a fireplace, but she just didn't use it. He'd have to keep that in mind.

"Where's Mason tonight?" she asked, looking around and then taking a chair across the table from where he stood.

He followed her lead and sat down.

"He's with my mom. They're decorating the house. He seemed to be kind of excited about it, which surprised me, because typically everything we suggest is shot down."

"I think he's turning around," Hannah said with a smile.

Somehow, her confidence in his son bolstered his spirit in a way nothing had in a long time. He loved that she believed in him. And he supposed Mason loved that too. He'd lost that somehow.

"All right, so let's get started," Hannah began, folding her hands with her notebook in front of her.

For the next two hours, they hammered out something that worked for both security and medical support for the Mistletoe Festival.

Hannah had a bunch of ideas that Ben thought were amazing, and he was impressed with how she had come to the table, not fighting to get as much money as she could for the medical side but trying to figure out how they could combine the two in a way that made sense for both of them. She was a real team player, and several times during the meeting, he found himself wondering if that was the kind of attitude she would bring to a marriage. It had been missing in his first marriage.

And he couldn't lay all the fault at his ex's feet. He had certainly had more of a competitive spirit than a "let's get along and see if we can help each other out" kind of thing. Because they were playing for the same team.

He was tempted to ask her if he could see her home, but he knew she had driven herself, and that seemed silly. Still, he was a little concerned about making sure she got there okay and almost asked if she would text him when she arrived safely, since he knew her place was outside of town. Still, he had no right to ask her to do that much, so they parted ways, and he walked home to his mother's house down the street.

"My goodness, that was a long meeting," his mother greeted him as he walked in the door. The place smelled like baking bread with just a little bit of cinnamon and sugar mixed in.

His mom was not perfect. She had a tendency to be a little bit pushy about getting her way, but she had a good heart. And while he knew she had been embroiled in a bit of a scandal having to do with donations the church had been accepting a few years ago, that wasn't who she truly was. And he ought to know, since he'd grown up with her. But after his dad had died, she'd been in a difficult situation, and him moving in and paying rent had eased her financial burden, and it had given him a place to land, keeping his son away from the bad influences that he'd begun hanging around with back in the city where they used to live.

"It took longer than I thought, but I think we have everything pretty well hammered out. We'll both need some help, but not for committee purposes, which surprised me."

"You mean you'll need help on actual festival day?" his mom said as she poured some water in a glass and handed it to him.

He hung his hat and coat up and accepted the glass with thanks.

"Festival day and the day leading up to it, since we need help setting up our booth and table and putting together a first aid kit and different security cameras. But I think we have everything mapped out. I wasn't expecting to get so much accomplished today."

"That Hannah, she always was a real go-getter."

"So you remember her from years ago when she used to stay here in the summer?"

"I sure do. Her gram was beloved by everyone, and while she was kind of quiet and never really seemed to spend a whole lot of time with friends in town, she was with her grandmother a good bit and was intelligent and well-liked by the adults in our group, if I remember correctly."

"Yeah. I remember her as very studious, and I suppose she was alone a good bit, but to be honest, I don't recall anyone ever going out of their way to invite her to do anything with us. We all went to school together during the year, and she was kind of an outsider."

"That's true. I do think she had more friends at the church she attended, which at the time, we were going to a different church. That helps if you see people in some kind of social situation where you get to know them."

Ben knew his mom was right.

"Where's Mason?" he asked, glancing around and not seeing him in the living room or sitting at the dining room table.

"He finished up his homework and then said he wanted to get to bed early because he didn't want to miss the bus again, since the school counselor, Kate, told him that in order for him to be able to do his work-study program at the medical center, he couldn't afford to be late to school anymore or he would jeopardize it."

Wow. Ben had to admit being rather surprised. It was only ten o'clock, and his son went to bed voluntarily?

Again, he had Hannah to thank for that. Sometimes he wondered if parenting wasn't more stumbling into the right people at the right time who took an interest in their child rather than any particular skill on the parent's part. At least that's how parenting seemed to end up for him. If he hadn't bumbled into Hannah, he would still be fighting with his son over pretty much everything.

"He did say that tomorrow you two were planning on going back down to the river and continuing to clear brush. He seemed to really like that."

"I did too. It was fun to spend time with him." He thought about his schedule. "I'm doing the early shift tomorrow, so we can definitely plan on it."

"If you'd like, I can make sure we have either a quick supper, or I can pack something up for the two of you to take and eat while you're doing it. It's up to you. I am home tomorrow with no committee obligations."

Ben smiled at his mom. Having people in the house seemed to have brought her back to life. He hadn't realized that she was getting a little bit depressed after his dad died, and maybe the house was just too big and lonely for her. She'd mentioned more than once how much she appreciated having them there.

"If we catch Mason in the morning, we can ask him his preference, but I think we can grab a quick supper and head out after that. Maybe early, right after he gets home from the medical center?"

"Yes. I can make sure it's on the table so that you guys can get out of here in good time." She paused for a moment and then she said, "I know you're an adult, and you might think I'm prying, but I am your mom."

Ben froze in the process of rinsing the glass out and putting it in the sink.

"You're not prying. You can ask whatever you want," he said. He really wasn't trying to hide anything that he knew of anyway.

"Well, Judy Hefner called me just a bit ago and said that she saw you and Hannah chatting on the porch. I know that Hannah is a really nice girl and everything, but she's a doctor. I think she might be a little bit out of our reach."

Wow. His mom was saying that Hannah was too good for him. Her own son.

He supposed her comment should have shocked him, but it really didn't. She had made comments like that all through his childhood and lifetime actually. Maybe he didn't think that she meant that there was anything wrong with him. She was just very aware of feeling less than around people who seemed to have accomplished a lot.

Looking back, he wondered if maybe he'd allowed those comments to color his attitude at times. Maybe that's why he'd never gone to Hannah when she had been there during the summer and talked to her. Maybe his mom had made comments and made him feel like he wasn't good enough, or she was better than them. Maybe that's where he had gotten that idea to begin with.

Maybe, unconsciously, he had been doing that with Mason.

"I think Hannah is a really great person, and maybe you're right that she's a little bit out of my league, because she is generous and has a beautiful heart, and is better at seeing the good in people than I am, but I don't think just because she's a doctor or just because she's accomplished things makes her better than me. I agree with our founding fathers—all men are created equal."

"Oh, I didn't mean it like that," his mom said.

He nodded and set the glass down with a clank. If she didn't mean it like that, he wasn't sure exactly how she did mean it, but he didn't ask.

"I'd really love to see you two get together. I guess... I guess I said it the way I did because I didn't want you to be disappointed if you don't. Which... in hindsight is probably not a very good way to go about it, is it?" His mother moved closer, and he put his arm around her shoulders.

"I suppose we all have things we can work on. I know it's a lot easier for me to be less judgmental about your parenting skills when I look at myself and see the mistakes that I've made. It's really easy to pick apart someone else when we haven't done it ourselves."

"I think that's your roundabout way of saying that I was an okay mom after all," his mom said, a little twinkle in her eyes as she looked up at him.

"Yeah. You were better than okay. You loved me, no matter how dumb I acted sometimes, and that definitely counts for something in my book."

"You were always a good son. And you're a good son now. And you have a really awesome son of your own. And... I'm so thankful you're here. I guess I didn't realize how lonely I was until the two of you moved in."

"Well, good. Because I'm happy to be here too." It was getting a little mushy, and it was making him a little bit uncomfortable, but his mother was smiling, and he didn't pull away. She really had done her best. And she definitely had made some sacrifices for him, which at the time, he hadn't appreciated or even noticed. That seemed to be the thing with parenting. It was a type of job that didn't get appreciated until years after it was done. In fact, a child had a tendency to really not appreciate their parents as they were going through the parenting process.

Well, he could correct it now, because his mom really was a wonderful person. And she might've been jumping the gun a little bit about things between Hannah and him, but it made him think about how much he admired and appreciated Hannah.

"Ben?"

"Yeah?"

"I just want you to remember one thing for me, okay?"

"What's that?"

"Life is shorter than you think it is."

Chapter Fourteen

Hannah hummed softly along to the Christmas music playing out of the speaker in her living room, as she hung another bulb on the tree.

All of her gram's antique Christmas decorations had been in the attic, and she'd been slowly bringing them down and putting them up in her spare time.

Outside, a few stray snow flurries fell past the front porch light, as the lights twinkled in her living room and the scent of her Cowboy Butter Meatloaf hung in the air. It had been one of her grandma's cherished recipes and, while Hannah's didn't taste exactly like she remembered, it had been pretty good.

Her tree was almost completely done, decked the way her grandma always had it, and it fit perfectly with her memories.

She smiled, glancing over at the Christmas town sitting on the buffet, which had been her favorite decoration of all time when she was younger.

In her memories, it was sparkling and beautiful and very valuable, but in reality, as she looked at it through the eyes of an adult, the sparkly ice was just aluminum foil, the figures in the town were plastic and probably cheap. But the warmth that it exuded, the glow of the lights in each tiny house, the snow-covered trees, and the little hill where one figure raced down on a toboggan still gave the warmth and charm of a small-town Christmas the way it had in her youth.

She stepped back, reaching for her hot chocolate and taking a small sip, savoring the sweet goodness as she studied the tree with approval.

Her gram would have been proud of her. She couldn't have done it better.

As "Deck the Halls" stopped playing and there was a pause between songs, she could hear the faint sound of a chainsaw.

Glancing at her watch, she saw it was almost nine o'clock and had been dark for several hours. But Ben and Mason were still down by the river, working with the lights from his truck headlights, she assumed.

The two had been at it every night that week except for one, which Hannah had learned the next day had been the night that Ben had needed to work late.

She was glad that she had been able to offer him something that he had been able to do with Mason, and Mason, for his part, had come into the medical center every afternoon full of things to talk about that he and his dad had been doing, the creation of a fishing spot on the river being the most exciting.

Although Mason had definitely enjoyed his time at the medical center and did every task he was given with an intensity that reminded her of his father.

Ben.

She smiled a little, thinking about their meeting earlier in the week and the few times that she'd seen him picking Mason up from the medical center.

It wasn't that far, and Mason could walk, and Mason had mentioned to her that he wasn't sure why his dad insisted on picking him up.

There was a part of her that hoped that Ben was doing it because he wanted to see her. Of course, that was a silly thought a schoolgirl might have, but she couldn't mature past them.

Because she hoped that Ben would come pick Mason up so that she could have a glimpse of Ben.

She hummed along with the melody to "O Little Town of Bethlehem" while she set the chocolate down and tidied up the boxes. She hadn't really thought about what a huge house this was and how one person kind of rattled around in it and how her grandma maybe had felt lonely at times.

Maybe her coming to stay with her grandma during the summers had been just as much of a joy to her as it had been to Hannah.

If her gram had said so, she didn't remember. All she remembered was that her grandma always looked happy to see her and always made her feel like she was wanted and loved.

Maybe when she had the house decorated, she would get out her grandma's old Christmas recipes and see if she could re-create some more of the things she remembered eating as a child and loving since the meatloaf had turned out so well. Things that made the holidays seem more like a holiday.

Of course, that was assuming she was going to have time, with getting ready for the Mistletoe Christmas Festival and doing some double duty at the medical center as Terry's time drew near.

She started thinking about children and work at the medical center and recipes and was surprised by a thump on her back porch.

What could that be? she thought to herself as she paused for a moment, then hurried to the door. She needed to get a dog. She was far enough out that it might be a good idea. She didn't want to do it around the holidays, though, but she made a note to think about it in the spring.

Glancing at the corner where an umbrella sat leaning against the wall, she decided she would use that as a weapon if she needed it as she opened the door and glanced out the crack before opening it wider.

"Ben?" she asked, surprised to see him standing on her porch, Mason beside him, grinning from ear to ear.

"We brought you some firewood. Dad said you didn't want to have a fire by yourself, but he also said that you didn't say you didn't want a fire at all, so he said we should stack some up on your porch."

"I know we kind of talked about it, and if you don't want it, we can take it back." Ben shifted uneasily on his feet, and she shook her head with a smile.

"Oh, it's fine. A fire would be perfect, and maybe there'll be a reason to have one; now I don't have an excuse not to." She glanced from Mason to Ben. "You guys can come on in, and I'll give you some hot chocolate."

"Maybe when we're done. We have enough firewood to make about three more trips each," Ben said, his brows raised as though asking if she wanted that much.

"That would probably be more than enough for me for the year and then some."

"Sounds good. Anything else we get, we'll make sure we give away to someone else."

"All right." She lifted her brows. "Twenty minutes? And I'll have hot chocolate waiting for you." She paused. "I have some cowboy butter meatloaf left from supper that I could warm up as well."

Mason's eyes lit up.

Ben grinned. "We're not turning down food and hot chocolate, apparently. We'll be in if it's not too much trouble."

She glanced at Mason's eager eyes and figured that the kid was a typical teen and hungry all the time.

"No trouble at all," she said. And she meant it. In fact, now the evening seemed much brighter, considering that she was going to have some company and she could serve them something that would warm their insides and make them smile.

She hummed along to "Joy to the World" as she bustled in the kitchen, heating some milk for the hot chocolate and getting mugs ready as the meatloaf warmed in the microwave. It was almost twenty minutes later when there was another knock at the door.

She went to answer it and was surprised to only see Ben standing there.

"Mason?" she asked, looking over his shoulder, even though the porch was completely deserted.

"There's one more load to bring up, and Mason asked if he could do it because he wanted to be able to drive the pickup. At that age, driving anywhere is a special treat." He blew out a breath as though he were nervous, but she couldn't imagine why he would be. "I can wait out here if you want me to."

"Of course not. Come on in," she said, opening the door wider so that he could come in.

He pulled his hat off as he did so and stepped in on the rug.

"Don't worry about the dirt. My grandma always used to say that she would rather have people here and show hospitality than have a clean house. I guess I never really thought about it, but I definitely feel the same."

"I think it's probably the biblical way to feel, although sometimes we tend to make our house a shrine."

"That's true. We're so worried about how it looks that we forget that it's supposed to be warm and welcoming, and people aren't supposed to feel put out or scared that they're going to break something."

"That's a cute miniature Christmas town," Ben said as they walked by her favorite decoration.

"That always makes my heart smile when I see it. Although I was thinking tonight how different it is looking at it through adult eyes. It was my favorite decoration when I was a kid and still is, but it looked so much more magical back then, you know?"

"Sometimes I wish I could still look at the world through a child's eyes. Because everything seemed a little bit simpler." He paused for a moment, as though weighing his words, and then he said, "Maybe it's just because I didn't have so much baggage."

"You talked a little bit about your divorce the other night, and I realize that I probably shared more with you about my termination from the hospital than I shared with anyone since I came. If there's anything you want to talk about...?" She let her voice trail off with a question at the end so that he could jump in if he wanted to. She had to admit she was curious, but also, sometimes it just helped to talk about things.

"I don't really—I guess I do feel guilty, but I wasn't the one who chose to cheat, you know? And you can't make someone love you when they've decided that they love someone else instead. Just standing there demanding it is fruitless. So I was handed a choice that I didn't want to make, and now I just have to make the best of it. My goal is to not be bitter and angry and allow that to affect my son."

"At least you're aware of it. I think a lot of parents aren't. They see their kids as weapons or pawns for their side, and they try to poison them against the other parent. It's so sad. It's like we never really grew up, you know?"

"Yeah. I'd like to have a little bit more than a first-grade mentality when it comes to dealing with my ex. Even if sometimes it feels like that's how she deals with me."

She felt bad for him. He didn't exactly look like he'd had his heart broken by her, but he looked like he'd had his heart broken because of the way it had upended his life.

A sound from the kitchen made her remember the milk that she had heating on the stove.

"Oh!" she said, turning so quickly she lost her balance and reached out to the wall to steady herself. At the same time, Ben reached out a hand to keep her from falling, and they ended up standing a good bit closer than they had been. She realized her breath was coming quickly as she stared into his eyes and couldn't seem to get her wits about her, to move, to do anything other than wait. But she didn't quite know what she was waiting for. For him to say something? Move closer? To reach up and touch his shoulder?

"Hannah." His voice sounded a little hoarse, like it was rusty and hadn't been used in forever, but there was also a tone of wonder in it, like he wasn't quite sure why they were standing there either, but she got the feeling that he didn't want to move any more than she did.

She didn't know how long they would have stood there or what might've happened when the door burst open and Mason said, "I got to drive the truck! It was pretty awesome!"

He slammed the door behind him, and by that time, Hannah had jerked back and moved around Ben, heading toward the kitchen.

She threw a smile over her shoulder that she hoped did not have any of the agonizing, uncertain feelings that swirled all through her chest.

"Perfect timing. The milk is ready, and all I have to do is stir in the chocolate."

Her voice sounded almost normal. Now if she could just get her heartbeat and breathing under control.

What *was* that?

She wasn't sure. Her hand trembled slightly as she stirred the chocolate in and then poured the thick liquid into mugs.

"Here you go," she said as she walked into the dining room with a mug in each hand.

"Don't you have any?" Ben asked, and if he had any lingering issues from whatever moment they'd shared, she couldn't tell. His hands seemed steady when he reached out to take the mug from her, and he was careful not to brush her fingers.

"I had some earlier, and I think that's probably enough for me."

"Thank you," Mason said as he took the mug from her and immediately put it to his lips, prompting her to say, "Careful, it's hot."

He blew on it a bit before he took a sip and jerked back.

"You're right." That's all he said, but there was a bit of a smile on his lips like he knew he should've listened instead of rushing ahead.

Maybe the kid was learning a little.

"Did Mason tell you about the unusual patient we had today?" she asked as she brought plates of meatloaf to the dining room table and indicated that both of them could sit down.

"No?" Ben asked as he followed her lead and sat down, deliberately choosing a seat on the other side of Mason so there was as much space as possible between them.

"Mason, do you want to tell him?"

"We had a dog!" Mason said, laughing, causing Ben to laugh.

"A dog?"

"Jan Weller's dog somehow ripped a hunk of skin on its leg and she brought it to us because the veterinarian was closed and didn't answer his emergency number. So we shaved it off and stitched him up and told her to go see the vet in the morning."

They chatted about that for a little bit, and then Mason had a few more stories, although he was very careful not to give out any medical information that would violate patient confidentiality.

Hannah made a note to mention to Terry that he was doing an excellent job of remembering what he had been taught and adhering to that.

They chatted about a few other things while the meatloaf and chocolate disappeared, but Ben and Mason did not stay long after that. Still, their visit left a glow that maybe wasn't entirely due to the fact that she'd enjoyed having company, as Hannah hummed softly to herself and washed the dishes in the sink later.

Ben was a really great man. She hoped she got to see more of him.

Chapter Fifteen

en walked along the street in Mistletoe Meadows, heading toward the gazebo.

Last night with Hannah had been perfect. Other than he wished it would've lasted longer.

He wasn't sure what was happening between them, but he remembered what his mom had said about life not being as long as what a person thought it was. And she was right.

He always thought he would do things later, some other time, when it was more suitable, when it worked out better, or he'd wait and see how things worked out. With Hannah, he felt like he was unsure whether or not it was the right time for his son. After all, Mason was still reeling from the divorce and feeling like his mother had abandoned him and his dad had taken him away from all of his friends. It wasn't the right time for Ben to get involved with another woman. Even if Hannah was interested.

Except... life wasn't as long as what he thought it was. And the time to do things was now.

Lord, I don't want to move too fast, but I also don't want to sit around when You've dropped the perfect woman into my lap, maybe thinking that it's not the right time. Your timing is better than mine. I just don't know what to do.

As though he'd conjured her up with his prayer, he realized there was a figure sitting in the gazebo, and it looked an awful lot like Hannah. Except it was early for her, and... what would she be doing there?

Was God answering his prayer that quickly?

And was that an answer, having the person he was praying about suddenly sitting in front of him when, as far as he knew, she had no reason to be there?

Saying a quick prayer that he would make the right decision and not say anything too stupid, he moved forward.

"I wasn't expecting to see you here this morning," he said.

She startled a bit, then recognition entered her gaze, and she smiled.

"That's funny. I was thinking about you this morning."

That was a good sign. He couldn't stop the grin that lifted his lips up. "You were?" He leaned against the pillar, putting one foot on the step and resting a hand on his thigh. He enjoyed looking at her, with her coat bundled up and a hat down over the top of her hair, which flowed out on either side. Her cheeks and nose were rosy, and her eyes sparkled as she sat with her hands in her pockets, her feet crossed at the ankle and tucked under the gazebo bench.

"Yeah. I probably shouldn't admit this, but I got up this morning thinking about how much I enjoyed last night, the hot chocolate, the Christmas music, having you and Mason cutting firewood and coming in to get warm and eat, and the idea of a fire in the fireplace. And... you. I enjoyed myself."

"I'm glad to hear it. It's nice to know you were thinking about me."

"So much so that I got up and got dressed and left for work and didn't even realize that I was about two hours early."

He laughed. So maybe she really was thinking about him, to the point of distraction. He liked that.

"I definitely had a great time, and Mason did too. He mentioned several times how much he likes you."

"He's a great kid. He's been doing a fantastic job at the medical center." She opened her mouth to say more, but "Jingle Bells" started pouring out of her pocket, and she said, "That's my phone. Excuse me."

He nodded and pushed off from the post, turning his back, shoving his hands in his pockets, and looking out over the town. Whoever had vandalized the gazebo had never been caught, and he'd been extra diligent while making his rounds. Of course, more than once he'd run into Secret Saint type people who were coming back from doing their good deeds. He dealt with Roland McBride, and didn't know a lot about it, other than the Secret Saint baton had been passed that year. After the spate of vandalism that had been happening, the people who were in charge of it had thought that he should know so that he wouldn't be suspicious of unusual activity that was actually aimed at helping people and not destroying the town.

He smiled. The new Secret Santa was the perfect person for the job. No one would ever guess who it was.

"Today? Now? Oh! That's so exciting!" There was a pause, and then Hannah said, "Of course. I'm more than happy to do that. I can take care of it." Another pause. "Oh no. No problem at all. That's what you hired me for."

There were a few more words, and then Hannah hung up.

By the time he turned around, she had shoved her phone in her pocket and stood up.

"It sounded like Dr. Terry might be having her baby," he guessed, assuming it was good news from the glow on her face as well as her smile.

He had to admit that he was a little bit disappointed, because he was on the verge of asking her out, but she had gone from being relaxed and chill to acting like she wanted to leave immediately.

"Yes, that's exactly right. And if you don't mind, I need to get to the medical center. She was going to meet me there with a few last-minute things that I need while they're on their way to the hospital."

"All right. I don't want to hold you up, and I certainly wouldn't want her to end up having a baby on the way, so I'll just say it was nice seeing you, and I hope to see you again."

She paused on her way down the steps out of the gazebo and looked over at him. He hadn't realized how much smaller than he she was—a good half a foot, at least. She seemed bigger, maybe because of her personality or because of the competence she displayed. He wasn't sure, but it kind of surprised him in a way. Not that he minded. She was the perfect size.

Their eyes met, and this time, he didn't stop his hand as it reached up and touched her shoulder.

She didn't step back, which he viewed as a good sign.

"I suppose you'll be extra busy for the next couple of weeks or more."

"Yes. We've been deliberately not scheduling appointments until after the new year, but all the emergency cases will be on my shoulders."

"With that and planning for the Christmas festival, I probably won't see you much."

"Probably not." Maybe it was his imagination, but he thought she looked a little disappointed.

"If you have time, maybe we could meet for coffee some morning before work, or hot chocolate in the evening?" He knew he should let her go—he'd told her he would—and he didn't want to keep her when she needed to leave. But he also wanted to confirm that whatever was between them wasn't going to totally die before they could see if it went somewhere.

"I'd like that. Friday evening? Seven o'clock?"

He grinned. He wasn't sure if he had just asked her out on a date or if she'd commanded him out on one. Either way, he wasn't going to argue.

"Seven o'clock, hot chocolate, at the Mistletoe Diner?"

"Yes, it's a date," she said. Then her eyes got big, and she clamped her mouth shut, like maybe she'd overstepped by calling their hot chocolate a date.

"It's a date," he confirmed, and her lips softened and curled into a smile.

His fingers slid down her coat, and he lost contact with her. It was just a second later when she finished going down the stairs and hurried off in the direction of the medical center.

He had a date. With Hannah.

Chapter Sixteen

he next few days were an absolute whirlwind for Hannah as she handled everything at the medical clinic by herself, with Terry in the hospital. Thankfully, the birth was uneventful, and they had a healthy baby girl whose two older brothers were excited to welcome her home.

Terry had mentioned to Hannah that she actually might be interested in hiring another doctor, one who might be willing to split part-time hours with her, who also had a family and would like to spend more time with them.

Terry hadn't found anyone like that, but she said she'd been praying about it and hoped that God had the right person out there. That meant Hannah would be the full-time doctor, with two part-time doctors working at the clinic as well. Hannah was okay with full-time hours, but somehow being around Ben had made her think that eventually she might want part-time hours of her own to raise a family. She'd definitely come full circle from her days where she thought her career was everything and she put sixty or eighty hours a week into it.

Friday couldn't come fast enough, and she practically hummed down the street, despite the fact that she was exhausted. It was the most she'd worked since she left her job in the big city, and she had to admit she wasn't used to those kinds of long hours. Not anymore. And she didn't want to go back to them.

She wanted... to her surprise, she wanted things she'd never wanted before. A quiet life. A cozy home with a loving husband and children running around. It seemed ideal in her head. Even after witnessing the issues that Ben had with Mason, she knew that there would be challenges with any children. Still, the idea of children and a family and building something that was full of laughter and love seemed much more appealing to her than having an illustrious medical career, even one that saved a multitude of lives.

Not that there was anything inherently wrong with that. She admired the people who did it, but now that she'd been yanked off of that track and dropped somewhere where she didn't expect to be, she could only think that it was God changing her life's direction.

She smiled as she got closer to the diner, seeing that Ben was already there, his hands shoved in his coat pockets against the chill of the evening, as a few stray flurries drifted lazily down.

He had been watching for her approach, and his eyes seemed to be glued on her as she got closer.

She liked the way he watched her, like he didn't want to take his eyes off of her, or more like he couldn't. It made her feel feminine and powerful in a not-arrogant but appealing way.

Like the attraction she felt for him wasn't one-sided.

"Good evening," she said as she got closer.

"Good evening. It's a perfect evening for some hot chocolate," he said with a grin.

"Yes, I could definitely use something to warm me up," she said, and then she laughed a little. "Or perk me up. It's been a long, busy week."

"I figured. Mason's been saying how busy you are. A couple of times I felt like maybe I should have let you off the hook for this evening, because I figured you'd be tired. But call me selfish, I wanted to see you." His eyes held hers, and she had no doubt he was sincere. His words warmed her straight to her bones, and she smiled.

"I wouldn't have let you cancel. I've been looking forward to it all week. I didn't care if I had to drag myself on my hands and knees, I was coming."

"I'm glad it didn't come to that," he said, turning and opening the door for her so she could walk in.

She murmured a thank you and lifted her face to the warm heat that blew over the top of the door as she stepped into the delicious scents of fresh-baked bread mingling with spices and herbs and chocolate.

"It smells delicious in here," he said from behind her.

"Boy, does it ever," she said.

It was a seat-yourself kind of place, and she turned, allowing him to lead them to a spot—a corner booth that was both cozy and intimate and right next to the window where they could watch the flurries, which were looking like they were getting a little more earnest as they began covering the sidewalk.

"Maybe the weatherman was right after all. I was starting to think that it was just wishful thinking when he said we were going to get four inches tonight," she said as she slid into the booth and shrugged out of her coat.

He laid his on the seat beside him and nodded. "I have an old injury in my left knee that usually hurts when we're going to get snow or any kind of weather. It was hurting all day today, so I kind of thought that they might've been a little off on their timing, but it was coming."

"Well, now I know I can just ask your knee if I want to know what the weather is going to be doing."

They laughed together.

"I was kind of hoping that it would be okay for me to actually get food along with hot chocolate. I just got off and haven't had anything all day."

"Oh, I'm sorry. Of course. I haven't eaten either, and if you don't mind, I'll do the same."

"I don't mind at all."

The menus were on their placemats, and she perused it while asking, "What about Mason? Has he eaten?"

"Mom's got him covered. I had told her that I'd be meeting you, and then I called her earlier this afternoon when I realized I wasn't going to be home in time to have supper either."

"I bet your mom loves having you there," she said, deciding on the hot turkey dinner. She was definitely in the mood for some warm comfort food.

"I appreciate her letting us come. With the divorce, I needed to sell the house, not only because I didn't have enough equity to buy it myself, but also because I needed to get Mason away from the bad influences that he was hanging around back in the city."

"I see." She appreciated what that showed about him. The sacrifice he was willing to make for his son.

The waitress came and took their orders, and then she picked up that thread of the conversation.

"I heard from someone that you were on track to be the police chief, and you left that job to take a huge pay cut and demotion by coming out here and working as a deputy sheriff."

"I suppose that's true. A demotion. I am overqualified for this job. And the sheriff's job is an elected position, so that was definitely out."

"Because you weren't able to be here in time to run?" she asked, assuming that's what he meant.

He shook his head. "I would never run to be elected. I... don't know anything about that. I'm just a cop, and that's really all I want to be."

"So you wouldn't consider running?" she asked, surprised. "That's a law enforcement position and you would be great at it."

"I suppose it is. I guess I just never considered it," he said, shrugging his shoulders.

But he looked like he was thinking about it now.

"I wouldn't even know how to go about getting started."

"Greg is a great guy, and I suppose if he were running again, I wouldn't recommend running against him, but if for any reason he decided to move on, I would definitely think that you should apply for the position. Not necessarily because I think you need to or anything, other than the town could use someone like you in a higher position. I think they would be foolish not to jump on the chance to vote for you."

He laughed. "Well, considering that you have just agreed to a first date with me, perhaps your opinion is a little bit biased."

"You're right. My opinion might be a little bit biased, but then again, maybe I just have really good judgment." She lifted her brows and grinned at him.

He laughed. "I'd like to agree with that, but it seems a little arrogant. No offence, but maybe you have really poor judgment."

Chapter Seventeen

Ben tried not to show his amazement. He hadn't even considered running for sheriff. He had just assumed that the deputy position that he had taken was what he was going to have as long as he lived in Mistletoe Meadows. But Greg had mentioned that he might be moving back to the DC area where he'd come from to take care of his aging parents, and while the implication there was that he was not going to be running in the next election cycle, Ben had just ignored it, considering that he wasn't the slightest bit interested in trying to run and get elected to any position. He'd never been interested in politics. But Hannah made him feel like maybe it was possible.

"I'll definitely have to keep that in mind." It made him feel like he could do it because she believed in him. It was crazy how just a few suggestions and a smile and that feeling of being able to do it just almost magically appeared.

Everyone should have someone behind them believing in them.

He thought about his son and how maybe that was part of the problem. He had expected his parents to stay together, providing that foundation for him, and it had thrown his whole world into chaos when he perceived that his mother didn't care anymore, even though it might not be entirely true. Although Peyton definitely had given off that feeling even to Ben. After all, if she cared about her family, wouldn't she have counted the cost of cheating and decided that it wasn't worth it?

"You know, I've been thinking lately," Hannah began, and he pulled his thoughts away. He didn't want to be thinking about Peyton now. Not with Hannah sitting across from him. He had been looking forward to this all week.

"About?" he prompted.

"About how I had considered that taking this job was just a little stop on my way back to the city and back into a career that was demanding and had the potential to be illustrious and huge, but... maybe it's Terry having a baby and deciding that she wanted to find another doctor to work part-time so she could stay home part-time and raise her family, or maybe it's just the small-town atmosphere, but I found myself shifting gears in my head and thinking that giving up a career is a small sacrifice in order to have a slower lifestyle, to be available for my friends and neighbors and a family." She lifted a shoulder and adjusted her placemat absentmindedly. "It's just something I've been thinking about. And I suppose you've already done that. Left your big career and the opportunity for advancement and awards and recognition behind. And you did it for your son. I admire that."

There was the difference. Peyton had looked at what she had and decided that it wasn't worth giving up anything for. In fact, she almost acted like she just wanted to throw her family away. While Hannah, on the other hand, saw the value and realized that the sacrifice would be worth it.

Suddenly, everything clicked together, and he knew for certain that any risk that he took to deepen their relationship would be worth it.

"I really admire you. I think a lot of us chase fame and fortune for far too long. Sometimes we never get that figured out. And sometimes when we do figure it out, it's way too late. I think you figured it out at exactly the right time, while I can't say that I necessarily figured it out. I was more forced into it."

She shook her head, huffing out an ironic laugh.

"I can't take the credit. I was forced into it as well. I told you that I made a mistake and was fired on the spot. And I had that whole mourning period where everything that I had dreamed about had gone up in smoke, and I missed it and wanted it back. I was forced into the slower lifestyle. I might not have seen the benefits if I hadn't been." She tilted her head and squinted her eyes as though she were thinking about it. "I struggle with that some, though, because to some people, it's a calling to be able to work long hours and save lives, to practice medicine in a way that is beneficial to a lot of different people, and I appreciate that dedication to their craft. If I ever get sick or anything happens to me, I would want to be able to have someone like that taking care of me, operating on me, handling my case. You know?"

"I get it. You think you're making the best decision, but you appreciate the people who have made the opposite decision, and just because you've made one decision doesn't make their decision wrong?"

He phrased it as a question, but he was almost positive that was what she was saying.

"Exactly," she grinned.

He loved her smile. It lacked any artifice and just seemed to light up the entire room. Or maybe it was just him. But he had a hard time taking his eyes off of it.

The waitress came, delivering their food, and after she left, Hannah waited for him to say grace before they began to eat.

"Do you think that you're going to be too busy to help with the festival?" he asked, noting the dark circles under her eyes and realizing that she probably was exhausted from the extra work she'd taken on.

"No. I have a few people lined up to help me, and I know this is probably crazy, but Mason's been such a huge help in the medical center. Of course, he's not doing anything with the patients, but he's just been really fantastic at picking up any slack he possibly can, and I really think he's going to have a great bedside manner as well."

It warmed his heart to hear the praise about his son and to realize that he seemed to have turned a corner and was maybe no longer in danger of falling in with the wrong crowd.

After swallowing, Hannah continued. "Regardless, Terry was a little bit early, and we did have some appointments this week. Things should slow down next week, and we might even have lulls in time because all we'll have are the emergency cases. Sometimes we go an entire day with only two or three people walking in."

"Wow. All right, I won't worry about you as much then, knowing that."

"You don't need to worry about me. I could've told you that earlier. We have been scheduling things so that she could take time off without it being an inconvenience to everyone in the community. We just were a little bit off on the timing. Babies come when they want to."

"I suppose they do." He hadn't thought about babies for a long time, and while he had really wanted more children and Peyton had been adamant about saying no to that, he hadn't considered adding to his family for years.

"Do you want children?" he asked, and then could've bitten his tongue. This was a first date, and even at that, Hannah had had a hard time even calling it a date. And here he was, asking her if she wanted children.

But if he scared her, she didn't let on. "I never had before. I guess if I thought about kids, they were something I wanted way off in the future, but I told you about the whole mindset shift I've gone through lately, and... yes. I definitely want kids. I want the warm home, the happy family, the love and laughter and all the good things." She rolled her eyes. "Even though I know that it's not all sugar and roses all the time. I'm not naive like that. I just... I want a family."

"I think that's a good thing. I think a lot of times families take a backseat to everything else. For years I wanted siblings for Mason, and Peyton wasn't interested."

"What about now?" she asked, and she held her fork midair, waiting on his answer.

"With the right person, yes. It definitely has to be the right person, because I tried this before with the wrong person, and it's heartbreaking and messy, and the ones that suffer are the kids."

"I definitely agree with you on that—that's who suffers the most, although I think the adults suffer as well. So... what does the right person look like?"

"Don't panic, but I think she looks an awful lot like you."

Chapter Eighteen

Hannah could barely breathe.

Her heart felt like it was pounding and about to run out of the diner, but her lungs just wouldn't work.

It was crazy. When had her whole life dream changed? She had wanted to become a famous and competent doctor, renowned for her skill and ability, but now, living here in this little town of Mistletoe Meadows, the one thing she wanted more than anything else was to be with Ben forever.

"I think I scared you," he said, and while his voice had tones of laughter, there was concern in his gaze.

"No. I was just thinking about how far everything has shifted for me. I couldn't think of anything that I want more. Suddenly my dream is not about becoming a wonderful doctor. It's about becoming something with you, here, in this crazy small town."

"Kind of grows on you, doesn't it?" he said, and she looked down to see his hand covering hers on the table. She stared at the picture for a while, his fingers longer and thicker than hers, which were more delicate and fit perfectly inside of his.

"What about Mason?" she asked, reality pushing its way into the dream state that she somehow had fallen into.

"I definitely want to talk to him, but my mom said something the other night that made me think."

"What was that?" she asked, curious.

"She said life isn't as long as what you think it is."

He let the words hang there, and she thought about them for a moment.

"I guess I can see that. We always think there'll be time later. We can put things off, but... that's probably not the best idea. And I'm definitely guilty of that. I put all the personal things that a person could possibly want to do aside as I pursued my medical degree and then my career."

"So I guess what I was saying about that—Mason needs to be on board, but I wasn't going to wait forever for him, you know? That's not fair to you, and it's not right. It's not a good idea in life. You don't know how much time you have. And it's probably not as long as you think."

"I agree. But I also agree that Mason's already been through a good bit, and I don't want anything with you and I to set him back at all, since he seems like he's coming around."

"Because of you. You're the one who suggested he work at the medical center, and that's made all the difference."

"You're spending more time with him," she offered.

"That's you too. You're the one who suggested we clear a place to go fishing down by the river on your farm."

He raised his brows, questioning her, and she nodded in agreement. He was right. It had been her idea.

"But you took initiative. You didn't have to."

"That's true." He laughed a little, as though thinking that her stubbornness in refusing to take all the credit was cute.

They chatted about a few other things as they finished up their meal and he paid the bill, and then they slid out of the booth and put their coats back on.

"I feel like I need to take you home."

"You don't need to feel like that," she said, not sure if he was saying that he wanted to or just that he felt weird ending a date by parting at the restaurant.

"I just don't like the idea that you're heading there by yourself. I know you've done it a million times before, but... I feel like it's my responsibility to make sure that you get there safely."

"I'll be fine. I can text you when I get there."

"Would you think I was being too much of a stalker if I asked if it would be okay if I followed you home?" He sounded humble, like he sincerely cared about her, and it made her feel warm and happy. Usually, she was the one who was caring for others, and it felt good to be on the receiving end.

"Of course not. But I'll have to insist that you come in for a cup of hot chocolate."

"All right. I accept."

They smiled at each other, and then he opened her car door, and she got in.

On the drive out to her house, she felt like she was basking in a warm, happy glow, unsure exactly what was going on with them, but knowing that she liked the direction they were heading, and the fact that he was going to talk to Mason meant that he was serious.

She definitely was.

Her phone ringing startled her. It took a moment for the name on the screen to register.

Stephanie Brunswick.

They'd done their residency together. She'd lost track of her a little bit since her move, but they used to be very good friends, especially since Stephanie was originally from North Carolina.

"Hello?" She picked up on the hands-free.

"Hannah! It's Stephanie. It's been a long time."

"Yeah. My goodness, how are you?"

"I'm great. I actually got a job in Raleigh as the head of pediatrics at the hospital there. It's a huge step up and definitely the direction I want to go with my career. But I was stopping in to see my grandmother, and I thought you were near her now. I heard through the grapevine that you are in Virginia now?"

"Yes. Mistletoe Meadows."

"I thought so. That's just a couple of hours from my gram's. But I don't want to put you out. I'm sure you're probably really busy."

"No. I'd love to have you." She was sincere. She really would love to see her friend. But she kind of cringed when she thought about the small town and her position as doctor at the medical clinic. It was a far cry from the prestigious position she'd had in the city the last time she and Stephanie had talked. Her career definitely wasn't on an upward trajectory.

She swallowed. Just a few minutes ago she had been exceptionally happy about that. But now... talking to Stephanie made her doubt everything she had been thinking. Stephanie was going to wonder what was wrong with her because she'd basically been demoted. And not just a little.

But she had loved what was happening in her life. She had been thinking it was the best thing that could possibly have happened. How did that all change in an instant?

She gave Stephanie some directions, and Stephanie told her approximately what time she'd be driving through. She hung up the phone, still not feeling the greatest.

She'd almost forgotten about Ben following her when the headlights flashed behind her as she pulled into the farmhouse driveway.

He followed her down, and she parked, keeping her hands on the steering wheel before turning her car off and opening the door.

Was this really what she wanted? Did she want to try her hand at getting back into the fast lane, resurrecting her career and realizing those dreams?

Or was this new Mistletoe Meadows dream really what she wanted?

Or maybe she was asking the wrong question.

Lord, I've always been about me and what I want. And there's a part of me—I can't deny it—that feels embarrassed that Stephanie is going to come and see that I'm not living up to everything that everyone thought I was going to be when I was in medical school and residency. But I want to do what You want. No matter what everyone around me thinks.

As soon as she said that, she felt a peace steal over her. She hadn't decided to come to Mistletoe Meadows as much as God had orchestrated the events that had led to this. And the knowledge that she was right where she was supposed to be, with who she was supposed to be with, settled over her like a warm, soft blanket as Ben got out of his truck and walked around to her.

She smiled, and before she thought about it, she shut her door, hurried to him and wrapped her arms around him.

He seemed a little shocked, since he froze for a moment. Then his arms went around hers as he said, "Well, I feel like we've been parted for weeks or months instead of ten minutes."

"A lot has happened in ten minutes," she said, her face pressed against his chest, and she breathed deeply of his warm, masculine scent.

"A lot?" he asked, sounding confused.

"I guess in my mind I've been around the world and back, and I was just praying that I would do what God wanted instead of what I wanted. And as I prayed that, I just felt such a peace settle over me that everything that has been going on is exactly the right thing. Even though it represents such a mindset shift for me."

"You were wondering whether you wanted to stay in a small town? Be a small-town doctor?"

"I wasn't really questioning it as much as I had some doubts." She pulled back but kept her arms around him. He felt so solid and warm and perfect, she didn't ever want to let go. "I got a phone call from someone I was with in residency. She's got a big new prestigious position at a hospital in North Carolina. Her career is on a fast upward trajectory, and I was a little embarrassed to think that she's coming to see me, and I'm definitely not anywhere near that."

Obviously her words had an effect on him. His face fell, and he loosened his grip around her, although his arms didn't drop.

"I don't want to hold you back if that's what you want."

"That's just it. I don't want to do what I want. I want what God wants. And as soon as I started praying about it, I just felt a peace that Mistletoe Meadows was right, you are definitely right, and this small town and my position here is exactly where I'm supposed to be. There's no doubt in my mind. I just wavered for a bit, you know?"

He nodded slowly, but his eyes searched hers as though he were trying to figure out if she really meant what she was saying.

It was probably instinct on her part, but she took her hands and cupped his cheeks. "Now, I feel like since I allowed you to follow me the entire way out here, I ought to get some kind of reward out of this." She lifted a brow at him and watched while her words sank in. She smiled as understanding slowly dawned over his face.

"A reward?" he asked, and she thought he pretty much knew what she meant.

"Yes. You owe me a kiss good night. After all, I did allow you to take me out, pay for my meal, and follow me home. It's the least you can do."

He grinned, and then he obliged the pressure from her hands and lowered his head slowly.

"There's something wrong with your logic, but I'm not going to argue," he murmured as he closed the space between them and kissed her gently at first, but then his arms tightened, and she wrapped hers around him, and it was quite a while before he lifted his head.

"I don't think that was enough payment," he murmured, his eyes still closed but his lips smiling.

"Me either," she said, matching his smile and wondering why she'd thought, even for a second, that a prestigious career and a big hospital could possibly hold a candle to what she had right now.

Chapter Nineteen

"So I was wondering what you thought of Dr. Reynolds?"

Ben tried his best to not look nervous or concerned about what Mason's answer was going to be.

It was Sunday afternoon, and they were spending the entire afternoon down by the river. He'd seen Hannah in church that morning with her friend, Dr. Stephanie Brunswick, who looked every inch the successful doctor, even though she had been dressed in church clothes and not scrubs, and there had been no white lab coats in sight.

He'd wondered again if Hannah was going to regret her decision to give up any hope of a big career and would be happy in Mistletoe Meadows.

Or was she going to be like Peyton and decide after they were married that she wanted something else?

He was jumping the gun, because they hadn't discussed marriage at all. But he supposed at his age, he wasn't interested in dating unless it led to that, and maybe he was crazy, but he thought that Hannah was the same.

For him, the only hurdle he had to get over was his son's permission.

"I think she's awesome. She's always teaching me new things. I learn something new every day. It's always interesting too. And she has great stories about when she was learning to be a doctor and even in school. Did you know that they cut up dead bodies?" Mason asked, sounding amazed.

Well, this wasn't exactly where he thought the conversation was going.

"I believe they're called cadavers."

"Yeah. That's what she said too."

"I guess I did know that. But it's not something I think about a lot," he said, trying to keep the irony out of his voice.

"Why? Hannah is a good influence on me. You're always talking about how I need to have good influences. You weren't going to make me spend less time in the medical center, were you?" Mason asked, pausing as he picked up the wood that Ben had just split and looking at his dad with concern.

"No. On the contrary, I was hoping we could spend more time with her." He paused and then took a breath. "I was hoping it would be okay with you if Hannah and I dated. I'm interested in her, and I guess I wouldn't date her lightly. I would be thinking about marrying her eventually."

Maybe that was too much for his kid, but he didn't see the point in pretending anything else.

Mason stood staring, holding the wood, although it seemed to be forgotten in his arms.

"Like Dr. Reynolds would be my mom?"

"Your mom will always be your mom. But... I guess she'd be like a second mom, yeah. Eventually. I haven't asked her yet, but I wanted to make sure it was okay with you first."

Mason's face had fallen, and he stared at the ground, his nose wrinkled a little, obviously thinking hard about it. Ben preferred that over an off-the-cuff answer that maybe didn't take everything into consideration.

Of course, Mason was not an adult, and it wasn't like he wouldn't change his mind a million times.

"Do you think she'll leave?" he finally asked, looking back up at Ben. "Do you think she'll decide that she doesn't like me after all?"

That cracked his heart. He hated the fact that was what Mason had taken away from the experience with his mom. That she would leave, and that it meant she didn't care for him.

He didn't want to defend his ex, and he didn't want to say anything that wasn't true. But he also didn't want Mason to carry around scars from what someone had done to him, and a parent had the power to hurt a child more than any other person in the world.

"Sometimes people do things and we can't control those things. It has nothing to do with us, and it has everything to do with them. I know that's a really hard lesson, and it's kind of hard to differentiate between what's their responsibility and what's our responsibility. But if someone leaves you or doesn't seem to like you, it's not necessarily your fault." He paused. "I'm not saying we can't always look at ourselves and try to be better, but when you're talking about a parent, it's not the child's responsibility to be the kind of person that will make a parent stay. Does that make sense?"

Mason's brows had drawn down, like he was thinking about what Ben had said.

"I guess so. You're telling me that it's not my fault that Mom left."

"Right. I could've been a better husband, I could've been a better dad, I could've been a better person, but that really has nothing to do with your mom leaving. She had to make the decision to do what she said she was going to do and fulfill her responsibilities. She chose not to. That's not our fault."

"I guess I understand. But you're right. I do wonder if sometimes —if I had been a better kid, maybe if I'd gotten better grades or hadn't caused so much trouble. There was a time I colored on the wall and one time I scratched the table with my knife—"

"Stop. All of those things are normal things that kids do. I could go on and on about the things I did too. But again, when people around you don't meet your expectations, that doesn't mean you get mad at them and leave. That means you love them anyway. And that's what we have to do. I guess your mom can decide if that's what she wants to do or she wants to do something else, and that's where we have to realize that we can't control her. We can only control ourselves."

"That makes sense. But I guess it doesn't really answer my question about Dr. Reynolds. Is she going to stay?"

"She's the kind of woman who does. Yeah." He hoped he was right about that. It was part of the reason why he felt like he was falling in love with her. Because she was the kind of person who did what God wanted her to do rather than what she wanted herself. She was also the kind of person who looked around to see who she could help rather than looking around to see how she could help herself. Those were two of the main things that he loved about her.

Did he love her? It seemed a little soon to think so, but the kind of love he was thinking about wasn't the kind the world thought of. It was deeper and better than that. He should tell her.

"I guess there aren't any guarantees in life. We can't say for sure that she will or she won't. We can only control ourselves."

Mason said the last two words with him, and they laughed.

"I guess what I was asking is if it was okay with you, I would like for Dr. Reynolds to eventually be part of our family. But you're part of this family too, and every decision I make affects you as well."

"If I say no, are you going to not date her?"

That was a hard question. He had told Hannah that Mason was just going to have to accept it, and he'd meant that, but he really wanted Mason to want it.

"I'd really like for you to like her and want her too. If not, I guess we'll have to cross that bridge, because your gram recently told me that life is shorter than what we think it is." He huffed out a breath. "That means you only have a small amount of time to do all the good that you can do, and you shouldn't waste any of your time doing bad things."

"Like keeping my dad away from someone that he could fall in love with and spend the rest of his life being happy with?" Mason asked, one brow raised.

Maybe his son was a little more mature than what he gave him credit for.

"If it's in the power of your hand to do good, you should do it,'" Ben said with a little grin. He was pretty sure Mason was just messing with him now.

"I can't think of anyone else I'd rather have in the family. We could talk about medical stuff all day long, all night long, and all weekend long. She could be here right now, and we could dissect a frog or something."

"I think frogs are hibernating right now," Ben said, picking the mallet up and putting another billet of wood on the stump where he was splitting it. "Plus, I'm a policeman, not a doctor, and there's a reason for that. Blood makes me dizzy."

"I'll have to make sure I tell Dr. Reynolds that. That could be a pretty good thing to have hanging over your head if, say, I get in a bad fight or something."

"I can control it. Don't think I can't." Ben swung the mallet down, and the wood split nicely in two. He loved doing manual labor like this. And he loved it even more doing it with his son. And even more than that was doing it with his son and having his son enjoy it as well. Who would've thought that working at the medical center would've turned his kid around so completely?

He knew it was the Lord working, but it was also Hannah allowing Him to work through her. He smiled at the thought.

Chapter Twenty

Stephanie left early Monday morning, and while Hannah had enjoyed her visit, she wasn't sad to see her go.

Stephanie had given her a hard time about not being more ambitious, but otherwise, they'd had a nice visit. The problem was, Hannah missed Ben. It hadn't been long since she had seen him, and she couldn't wait until he came to pick up Mason so she could at least get a glimpse of him.

She couldn't remember ever being this head over heels for someone, and she laughed a little at herself for being such a schoolgirl. She was in her mid-thirties. She shouldn't be so silly.

But as she flipped the sign over on the door and turned the lights out in the waiting room, she couldn't keep from glancing out the window up and down the street, checking to see if he was on his way.

Usually, he was there five or ten minutes before they closed so Mason didn't end up waiting on him.

"Dad's not here yet?" Mason said, sticking his head out of the number two exam room where he was wiping everything down with a disinfectant wipe.

"No, not yet," she said. Before the words were out of her mouth, headlights splashed across the window.

"Never mind. There he is," she said, smiling as his truck pulled into the lot.

Trying to think of an excuse to see him more, she wracked her brain as to whether or not there was anything she needed to talk to him about regarding the festival. Everything had pretty much been hammered out, and they were ready for it to start next week.

She almost missed the giggling that came from the exam room where Cassie had now joined Mason.

Ben had almost made it to the door, but she turned, suspicious.

"What's going on with you two?" she asked, trying to look into the exam room to see if something had happened.

"Hey there, I've missed you," Ben said as he walked in.

"I missed you too. It's only been a day, which is crazy."

"I almost stopped in last night after we were done at the river, but you had company, and I didn't want to intrude."

"You would've been welcome," she said, stepping over and wondering if it would be too much to greet him with a hug. She had done that the last time when he'd followed her home, but it just seemed a little bit more public here, and she wasn't sure what the protocols were or even where their relationship was.

Although she'd been spending a good bit of time thinking about their kiss.

"You guys are under the mistletoe!" Mason jumped out of the room, his hand pointing toward the ceiling.

There was mistletoe? Her eyes met Ben's before they both looked at the ceiling. Sure enough, taped to the ceiling was a little sprig of plastic mistletoe.

"I guess you know what that means," Cassie said, laughter in her voice.

"You two planned this, didn't you?" Hannah said, realizing now what the giggling was for.

"Dad asked me yesterday if it would be okay if he dated you. I figured I should give him a little nudge, because Dad can be pretty slow sometimes."

"Oh, he can?" Hannah asked, wondering if Mason knew that his dad might be a little quicker than what he thought, considering that he'd already kissed Hannah quite thoroughly on Friday night.

"Yeah. I figured it'd be next year this time before he got around to kissing you. So I got the school counselor to let me borrow the mistletoe she had sitting on her desk. I told her it was for a good cause."

"I guess that means I need to kiss you. I just can't see any way out of it, can you?" Ben said, acting like a martyr, but there was a gleam in his eye that told her that he was not the slightest bit upset.

"I take it that your talk with Mason went really well," she murmured as he lowered his head to hers.

"Better than I thought," he said, pausing before his lips touched hers. "I love you."

She blinked. She was not expecting that, but her answer was easy. "I love you, too."

They shared a small smile before his lips pressed into hers.

They had an audience, so it wasn't a long kiss and wasn't nearly as good as the one on Friday night, but it was Ben, and she was just happy to be with him.

This would be the rest of her life. She was looking forward to it.

Join Jessie's list and be the first to know about new releases and sales on her books!

Read *Silent Night Dreams*, the next book in the Mistletoe Meadows series, where a deaf musician and a music shop owner discover that the most powerful songs aren't always heard—they're felt. Can a shared love of music help them find harmony, hope, and home? Keep reading for a sneak peek now.

Sneak Peek of Silent Night Dreams

"Ten minutes until showtime."

Grace Dempsey looked up at the stage assistant, the comb clutched so tightly it bit into her hand.

"Thank you so much," she said, inclining her head graciously, pleased to note her voice did not tremble.

"The crowd is sold out. There are people standing in the back! I've never seen it this packed!" The stage assistant's cheeks were flushed, and he clasped his hands together, giving her the kind of look that was usually reserved for mega rock stars or A-list movie stars.

Not a classically trained concert pianist like herself.

She waited until the door closed before she allowed the starch in her back to drain out, and she slumped down, deliberately setting the comb down on her dressing table.

You've got to get it together. Everyone is expecting to see a performance like last time. You can't let them down.

She had no sooner thought that than cramps squeezed her abdomen painfully, and she only hesitated a moment before she jumped up from her seat, running to the restroom.

She barely made it in time. But it didn't take long because she'd already emptied out everything in her digestive system from both ends. Her hands slid on the doorway as she leaned against it, her knees shaking, her forehead hot and clammy, hands cold and clammy.

How was she going to go out and perform? She couldn't even sit at her dressing table without having to run to the restroom.

And what was wrong with her? She'd never had this kind of problem before. She'd always been eager to perform, excited. She looked forward to it.

But today, today, she was scared to death to go out in front of that huge crowd.

Everyone was expecting her to be able to play like she had last time. And the time before that. And the time before that. And she could, she knew she could. She just had to play the way she always had.

Except that the idea of going out made her turn right back around and head back into the restroom.

She couldn't go out like this. There was just no way.

But she couldn't cancel. Not at this late moment.

Her phone buzzed, and she finished washing her hands, drying them on the towel and noticing that they shook so badly she could barely hang it back up.

On trembling legs, she walked back out into her dressing room and picked up her phone.

It was her manager.

Clearing her throat, she stared at her phone. Could she tell Sasha that she couldn't go out on stage? It would be unheard of for her to cancel at such late notice, unless there was a serious problem, probably requiring hospitalization. If she wasn't dead, she would perform. That's the way she'd been brought up, that was her mindset, except...

She took a deep breath. What was wrong with her?

Her hands trembled and she almost dropped her phone. How could she hit the notes with her fingers shaking so hard?

Finally, she swiped and put the phone to her ear.

"Hello?" she asked, in the cultured, casual tone that she always used. To her ears, it didn't sound like anything was wrong. How could she fake it so convincingly and yet be so utterly sure that she absolutely could not go out on stage?

"Grace. I just wanted to let you know that the president has made a last-minute decision to attend. He is settled in his seat, and he is looking forward to your performance. I just spoke with him, and he gushed over your last concert. He has several members of his cabinet with him, and they are eager to hear our American talent."

Grace swallowed hard, but she knew she wasn't going to be able to hold down the dry heaves for long.

"I can't." The words came out choked, as much as she would like to have continued to be able to speak in her unaffected tone.

"I'm sorry?" Sasha said, like the idea that Grace might have said that she couldn't do it was absolutely ludicrous.

"I'm sorry. I want to be able to, but I absolutely cannot." At least she had gotten better control of her vocal cords. Why couldn't she have been a singer?

But she still couldn't go out on that stage. The idea of performing in front of all of those people made her feel like her knees were going to collapse, and she felt hot and cold and absolutely petrified, like she needed to go hide somewhere. Without even thinking about it, her eyes darted about the room, looking under the chair, trying to figure out if she would fit there.

She was a grown woman. What was wrong with her?

"What?"

"I said I can't."

"I'm sorry, you can't what?" Sasha said, still obviously having trouble grasping the reality.

"I cannot go out on stage. You're going to have to cancel the concert."

Where would she go? What could she do? If she canceled this... She could still make next week's performance, except... The idea of performing anything made her feel like her throat was rotating like helicopter blades, and her stomach was attached for the ride. She needed to get out of here. She needed to escape.

"Are you sick? Should I call an ambulance?" Sasha asked, her concern reaching through the phone.

Sasha was not coldhearted, but she was not going to understand that Grace was pretty sure all this was, was a panic attack.

"Yes. An ambulance."

There, she'd admitted it. She felt a touch of relief, but mostly, admitting it had allowed it to have the upper hand, and she sank to the floor.

"I need an ambulance," she managed to grind out.

"All right. I'm hanging up right now and I'm calling an ambulance, and then I'll be right there. Five minutes tops. Hold on."

The phone went dead, and Grace allowed her head to rest on the cold floor. It didn't really make her feel better, but at least the heavy, suffocating weight of the thought of going out in front of all those people was no longer in the forefront of her mind, and she slowly felt like her insides were calming down. Her chest only ached a little, and she no longer felt like she needed to stay in the bathroom indefinitely.

What had happened? Was that what stage fright was? Could she go through with her performance anyway? If she tried to go out, would she have some kind of attack while she performed? Or should she just assume that once she started playing she would feel better.

The idea made her stomach clench again, and she shook her head quickly, although she was alone in the dressing room. Absolutely not. She couldn't start playing, not when there was a chance that she would end up with some kind of attack. Maybe she really was having a heart attack. She had heard that sometimes symptoms presented themselves differently in women than in men, and her chest really did hurt.

She only had a few more seconds to herself before the door burst in and Sasha hurried over, kneeling at her side.

"What's the matter?" Sasha asked, breathless.

"I think I might be dying. Heart attack? A stroke? I'm not sure, but I'm scared. And I feel terrible. Like Doomsday is here." That was a little dramatic, but it was the truth. She felt like she was going to die.

"Hold on. The ambulance is here now, and I have Penny bringing them back. They'll be here in a m—"

She didn't get to finish her sentence before the door burst open, without even a perfunctory knock. Grace couldn't remember the last time someone had come into her dressing room with such disrespect, except that she'd given into the fear, and she was overwhelmed by it. There had to be something seriously wrong, something life or death. It was a heart attack, or some kind of fast-growing cancer, or something. There had to be something wrong.

Sign up for Jessie's newsletter! Get a free book, access to exclusive bonus content, get fun and funny updates on her life on the farm and more!

A Gift from Jessie

View this code through your smart phone camera to be taken to a page where you can download a FREE ebook when you sign up to get updates from Jessie Gussman! Find out why people say, "Jessie's is the only newsletter I open and read" and "You make my day brighter. Love, love, love reading your newsletters. I don't know where you find time to write books. You are so busy living life. A true blessing." and "I know from now on that I can't be drinking my morning coffee while reading your newsletter – I laughed so hard I sprayed it out all over the table!"

Claim your free book from Jessie!